SYD

In the decades-old [...] between the world's [...] est gem dealers, the B[...] stones and the H[...] monds, no one and no- where is off-limits. Not even Danielle Hammond, the up-and-coming jew- elry designer who thought she'd escaped family hi- jinks up north in the Port Douglas tropics.

The flamboyant Dani has been hired by broker Quinn Everard to design for him—the same man who some time ago near- ly destroyed her fledgling career with his caustic cri- tique of her work. What would make the colorful Ms. Hammond agree to that unique assignment? And just who is Quinn's mysterious client?

The Blackstones and Hammonds, no strangers

rumors abound that the missing son of recently deceased founder Howard Blackstone may indeed have been located.

Before his death, How- ard—dubbed "the man people love to hate"—left his billion-dollar diamond firm to the missing son, James, who was kidnapped over thirty years ago. Tempers are high at Blackstone's Pitt Street offices—where the diamonds are rare, but the drama is rampant!

Dear Reader,

I love this job.

For this project, I revisited Port Douglas in northern Queensland, Australia. I again experienced the most beautiful stretch of beach, friendly people, a gorgeous winter climate and the superb restaurants in this small town that bats way above itself. Until we meet again, Port....

I have never been particularly enamored with the "girl's best friend." I am now! Via books and the Internet, I read about diamonds, from the mines to the perplexing world of the sightholders, and to the cutter's desk. I learned about the world's most famous diamonds—centuries old, desired by all, cursed for all time. I discovered big money, blood money and seductive marketing. I especially loved the beauty, diversity and astonishing prices of natural colored diamonds. My heroine is a jewelry designer, so I checked out hundreds of incredibly talented designers' sites and drooled over the most beautiful jewelry. And I was lucky enough to see firsthand how a vision is created.

I am a convert. To me there is no gemstone more steeped in power, greed, beauty, love—and yes, curses—than the immodest diamond.

Best regards,

Jan Colley

JAN
COLLEY

SATIN & A
SCANDALOUS
AFFAIR

Published by Silhouette Books
America's Publisher of Contemporary Romance

Thanks to Richard Baird of Rohan Jewellery in Christchurch, New Zealand, who spent hours sharing his knowledge and passion for diamonds and let me peek over his craftsmen's shoulders, and to Max Rooney of Argosy Jewellery for the introduction.
To our intrepid editor, Melissa Jeglinski, who must have experienced a few conniptions with this project. And special thanks to a great bunch of girls: Bronwyn Jameson, Tessa Radley, Maxine Sullivan, Paula Roe and Yvonne Lindsay. Long live Desire Downunder!

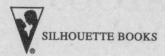 SILHOUETTE BOOKS

ISBN-13: 978-0-373-76861-5
ISBN-10: 0-373-76861-3

SATIN & A SCANDALOUS AFFAIR

Books by Jan Colley

Silhouette Desire

Trophy Wives #1698
Melting the Icy Tycoon #1770
Expecting a Fortune #1795
Satin & a Scandalous Affair #1861

JAN COLLEY

Jan Colley lives in Christchurch, New Zealand, with Les and a couple of cats. She has traveled extensively, is jack of all trades and master of none and still doesn't know what she wants to be when she grows up—as long as it's a writer. She loves rugby, family and friends, writing, sunshine, talking about writing, and cats, although not necessarily in that order. E-mail her at vagabond232@yahoo.com or check out her Web site at www.jancolley.com.

THE HAMMOND~BLACKSTONE FAMILY TREE

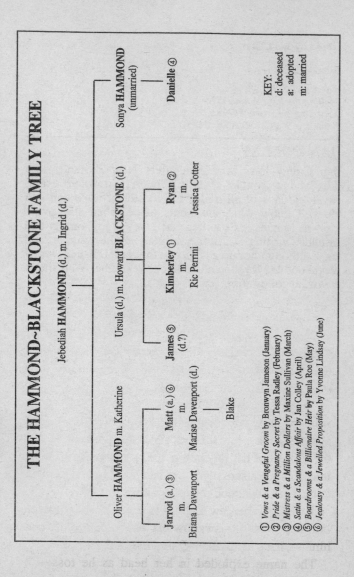

Jebediah HAMMOND (d.) m. Ingrid (d.)

Oliver HAMMOND m. Katherine

Ursula (d.) m. Howard BLACKSTONE (d.)

Sonya HAMMOND (unmarried)

Jarrod (a.) ③
m.
Briana Davenport

Matt (a.) ⑥
m.
Marise Davenport (d.)

Blake

James ⑤
(d.?)

Kimberley ①
m.
Ric Perrini

Ryan ②
m.
Jessica Cotter

Danielle ④

KEY:
d: deceased
a: adopted
m: married

① *Vows & a Vengeful Groom* by Bronwyn Jameson (January)
② *Pride & a Pregnancy Secret* by Tessa Radley (February)
③ *Mistress & a Million Dollars* by Maxine Sullivan (March)
④ *Satin & a Scandalous Affair* by Jan Colley (April)
⑤ *Boardrooms & a Billionaire Heir* by Paula Roe (May)
⑥ *Jealousy & a Jewelled Proposition* by Yvonne Lindsay (June)

One

"Danielle Hammond? I have a proposition for you."

Dani blinked, jolted out of a pleasant daydream, the Northern Queensland sun that had been warming her face at the outdoor café now hidden behind a wall of a man.

"May I join you?" The softly spoken deep brogue sounded more continental than Australian. She blinked again. It took a few seconds for her to understand that the subject of her daydream, the man she'd seen walk into her shop just minutes ago, had now crossed the road to the café and stood towering above her.

It took another few seconds to realise that she'd seen him before, and to swallow her jolt of dismay. It was him—what's his name—Quinn Everard!

The name exploded in her head as he tossed a

business card on the table and pulled out the flimsy white chair opposite her.

Dani eased her sunglasses down her nose and needlessly read the card. "Quinn Everard. Broker." Simple, classy, on a satiny-silver card. They'd never met personally, but she'd seen his face in many jewellery publications over the years.

His head turned toward the café door and immediately a waitress materialised. He ordered coffee while Dani's curiosity ran riot. What could the great Australian gem expert want with her? He'd made it very plain, very publicly, that she wasn't good enough to wipe his shoes on.

"Did you see anything you liked?" she asked, sipping on the straw of her thick shake.

Chocolate brown eyes under thick brows scanned her face.

"In the shop," she qualified, easing one hot foot out of her shoe under the table.

"I was looking for you. Your assistant pointed you out."

"You were checking out my window. I saw you."

He rested his elbow on the table and subjected her to a leisurely inspection. Just another nail in his coffin, as far as she was concerned. Dani stared boldly back, seeing in her mind's eye his tall broad form as he'd scrutinised her display window. How she'd admired what looked like an Armani suit—a rarity in the tropics—and his smooth, rolling gait as he'd straightened and disappeared inside. He moved like a fighter, and who's to say he wasn't? There was a definite break in his nose, the telltale bump high on the bridge, and a scar, smooth and pale, traced the corner of his mouth.

His inspection completed, he sat back in his seat. "I've been hearing your name around lately."

Thanks to Howard Blackstone, Dani's benefactor, who'd nominated her as his featured designer for the annual launch last February. "The Blackstone Jewellery launch, probably." Blackstone Jewellery was one retail division of Blackstone Diamonds, Howard's mining and manufacturing company. Dani pursed her lips sardonically. "Oh, I forgot. You weren't invited."

A flicker of amusement deepened the creases on both sides of his mouth, showing up an unexpected dimple. "I've never said I don't find your work interesting, Ms. Hammond. Which is why I'm here. As I said, I have a proposition for you."

She relished the sharp stab of triumph. This man had never made a pretence of liking her stuff, yet here he was. What on earth could he want to proposition her about?

Dani could think of some things…and they were all tied up with sizing him up as a hunk a few moments ago, before she'd realised who he was.

Hopeful that the lick of attraction she felt wasn't written all over her face, she cleared her throat. "A proposition for *me?* April Fools was a couple of days ago."

"I want you to design a setting for a large and very special diamond."

This was very satisfying. The great Quinn Everard wanted her, Dani Hammond, to make him a diamond necklace.

Oh, but there was that one small problem. They hated each other.

She raised her head. "No."

His eyes narrowed.

"Diamonds aren't really my specialty." His words, aimed at her four years ago at the prestigious Young Designer of the Year Award competition, the one everyone tipped her to win, came back to her. He'd said something along the lines of "A jewellery designer should stick to what she knows and is comfortable with. Ms. Hammond may have cut her teeth on diamonds, but she has little flair and understanding of the essence of the stones."

That wasn't the only public dressing-down Dani had received from Quinn Everard. She'd assumed it was because of the spat between he and Howard years ago.

"Remember?" she asked sweetly, and received a coolly assessing gaze in response. How could he sit there in his gazillion-thread suit and not melt?

"I am offering a generous commission."

Now, that was interesting… "How generous?" A little extra cash and she could make the final payment on her loan from Howard. Of course, she'd repay his estate, since he'd died earlier in the year. Generous enough to include some new display cabinets, maybe? A face-lift for the tired signage?

Quinn took out what looked to be a solid-gold pen, wrote something on the business card and turned it around so she could see.

A surprised cough escaped and she jerked her head up at the numbers on the business card. "You want to pay me that to make you a piece of jewellery?"

He nodded.

The amount was obscene. Damn the spruce-up. This could be the deposit for the bigger, more modern and vacant premises two doors down.

"That's way over the odds. You know that."

"Yes or no?"

She shook her head, positive she was the butt of someone's joke. "The answer's no."

Quinn leaned back, not attempting to cover his displeasure. "You and your family have endured quite a bit of unwelcome publicity lately, haven't you? Howard's death three months ago. Not to mention his companion on the plane."

Tell her something she didn't know. No one survived when the flight Howard Blackstone had chartered to take him to Auckland one night in January, plunged into the sea. When it turned out Marise Hammond was on board, the media were beside themselves. Marise was married to Howard's arch enemy, Matt Hammond, head of House of Hammond, an antique and fine jewellery company in New Zealand. Matt was also Dani's cousin, although they'd never met because of the feud between Howard and the Hammonds that spanned three decades.

The reading of Howard's will a month later rocked the family to its core. Marise was named as a substantial beneficiary and a trust fund was set up for her son, Blake, giving rise to the assumption that Marise and Howard were having an affair. Who was Blake's true father, everyone wanted to know, Howard Blackstone or Matt Hammond? All the old family history and hostility had been bandied around for months.

Despite a growing anxiety, Dani feigned nonchalance. "So?"

"And poor Ric and Kimberley," he continued. "They must have been bummed when the TV cameras crashed their wedding."

That was an understatement. Dani grew up in Howard Blackstone's mansion, along with her mother and cousins, Kimberley and Ryan. Kim had recently remarried her ex-husband, Ric Perrini. Their lavish wedding on a yacht in Sydney Harbour was nearly ruined when the media sent in helicopters.

What did Quinn Everard know about that?

"I haven't officially met Ryan," Quinn resumed, "but I do know Jessica slightly. I think she'll make a lovely bride, don't you?"

She opened her mouth to agree, then snapped it closed. Ryan and Jessica had recently announced their engagement, but the wedding details were a closely guarded family secret.

"I have no idea what you're talking about," she said warily.

Ryan was the most private of people. That's why he'd asked Dani to help arrange a secret ceremony up here, away from the Sydney gossip-mongers. Port Douglas was an excellent choice. Chances were, the family members wouldn't be recognised, and there were any number of world-class venues and caterers to choose from. With Dani's help, arrangements for the perfect intimate wedding in three weeks' time were well under way.

"Really?" Quinn mused. "There are some lovely beaches up here, aren't there? I hear Oak Hill is nice."

Dani's heart sank. He couldn't possibly have found out. Almost everything had been confirmed and all participants sworn to secrecy. "Your information is out of date, Mr. Everard," she lied. "There won't be a wedding in Port Douglas, after all. That was just a ploy to get everyone off the scent."

"A ploy? My source seems adamant that on the twentieth of April, the van Berhopt Resort is staging a very special event. It looks fantastic on the Web site, just the place for an intimate, discreet family wedding."

She heard the sound of her own teeth grinding. "How the hell did you know that?"

He tapped his nose. "The diamond world is surprisingly small."

Dani knew when her back was against the wall. "That's blackmail," she muttered.

He shrugged, all traces of amusement gone. "It's business, Ms. Hammond. Are you so successful you can afford to turn down a commission of this size?"

Intimidation really got her back up. "Do your worst." She pushed her glass away and picked up her purse. This was precisely why she had chosen to live up here, away from the city gossip. "The Blackstones and I are used to media attention." Howard's womanising and close-to-the-edge business dealings guaranteed that.

Quinn stroked his chin. "Poor Ryan and Jessica, their beautiful day ruined. And the rest of your family—especially your mother—will they be so blasé? All that distasteful speculation, old family wounds reopened, over and over…"

"Leave my mother out of this," Dani snapped. That

was the worst of it. The Blackstone-Hammond feud had ripped her mother's blood brother away from her thirty years ago, leaving a massive heartache. With Howard's death, Sonya Hammond's dearest wish was to bring the family factions together again.

"I can empathise, being a private person myself." His tone was sympathetic—reasonable, even.

Dani jutted her chin out defiantly, despite a sinking feeling that he was right. Did she have the right to expose those closest to her to more scandal and shame?

"You could spare them all that unwelcome attention. Ryan and Jessica will have the day of their dreams. And you, Danielle, will make a lot of money."

She glared at him. Only her family called her Danielle. Up here in Port, as it was affectionately known, she went by Dani Hammond, the brand name for her jewellery. Most of the locals had no idea she was connected to one of Australia's richest and most notorious families. Those who did, didn't care.

Quinn shifted impatiently. "Yes or no?"

Could she bear her anonymity here to be shattered by all the old gossip and innuendo she had lived with all her life? And worse, how could she let him ruin Ryan and Jessica's day and put that hunted look back in her mother's eyes? "Bring your damn diamond to the shop, then." Grasping her change purse in a white-knuckled grip, she stood abruptly and scowled down at him.

Quinn Everard tilted his head, peering up under his brows again. Then he rose, gesturing to the cars parked across the street. "My car is right over there. Take a ride with me."

Her internal alarm sounded. It wasn't that she thought a man with his reputation would try anything dangerous. It was her reaction—her attraction—that worried her. And how could she refuse a man who held such sway in her profession, especially one offering dream money?

"I don't carry this diamond around in my pocket." Quinn frowned at her hesitation. "I've rented a house in Four Mile Beach."

Four Mile was an outlying district in the shire of Port Douglas, and where her apartment was. "I'm working."

"Exactly. Time is money, Danielle."

She eyed him moodily, weighing her options. "Whereabouts in Four Mile?"

He impatiently motioned her to start crossing the road.

"You may be famous," Dani said tightly, "but you're a stranger to me. I'm going nowhere without telling my assistant."

He inclined his head. "Number 2 Beach Road." He stopped beside a sleek black BMW. "I'll wait."

Taut with indignation, she poked her head into the shop and told Steve, her assistant, and told him where she was going. Then she got into Quinn's car. They spoke little on the short drive, but her eyes widened in surprise when they pulled up outside his house. She'd walked past here nearly every day on her way to work. Never a morning person, she needed the fifty-minute walk along beautiful Four Mile Beach to improve her mood.

The house was right on the sand dunes, surrounded by high walls. A discreet plaque on the wall by the entrance said Luxury Executive Accommodation. Dani had always wondered what it was like inside.

She followed Quinn through the gate and entrance into a large multilevelled living and dining area. The house was a blend of Asian and Australian designs, the furnishings rattan, leather and teak. Striking floral arrangements with birds-of-paradise and heliconias seasoned the air with tropical scents, stirred by lazily rotating ceiling fans. This place was even better than she'd imagined.

"Shall we?"

Quinn stood at the door leading to the stairs. Dani hesitated for a second. She didn't trust Mr. Quinn Everard one inch, but it wasn't a threat of physical violence that made her pause. More his attitude, the impression that he got what he wanted so effortlessly. He smelled good, looked good, obviously lived well. She'd need her wits about her with a man prepared to resort to blackmail to get his own way.

He opened the first door and intense light flooded what was obviously a dream workroom. In one corner, under the perfect lighting, sat an easel. A workbench ran fully down one side, two stools at the end and tool organisers that held an array of implements, everything from tweezers to gauges to loupes. There was a waxing station, engraving blocks, micro torch, rollers and grinders—everything she had in her shop, except the equipment was new and top-of-the-range and must have cost a fortune.

It slowly dawned on her that he expected her to work on his diamond here. A laptop sat open on a desk, no doubt with the best CAD software available. The desk and bench were lit with magnified true-light lamps. He must have had all this brought in, she thought dimly, lights included.

Dani ran her hand over the workbench. "You were that sure I'd agree?"

"I've questioned your motivation in the past, Ms. Hammond, not your intelligence."

She glanced over to where he leaned casually against the doorjamb, arms folded. "Why?"

"The diamond does not leave the premises."

"So I come around here when I feel like it? When I have a spare minute?" She shook her head. "That would take months."

Quinn turned to the door and stretched his arm out, indicating she precede him. His steady gaze challenged her to refuse.

Cautiously Dani edged past him, down the hall away from the stairs. She paused at the next door. He leaned past her, pushing it open, and she took a couple of hesitant steps forward.

Long white curtains stirred at the open window, and she heard the sea lapping the sand beyond the trees. A huge bed, covered with shiny satin in bold red-and-gold stripes, took up most of one wall. Purple-shaded lamps on the bedside tables matched plump purple cushions scattered on the window seat. Dani felt the smile start; it was a dream of a bedroom, and to think she could hear the sea. She was still smiling when she turned around to see Quinn in a long-legged lean against the doorjamb, arms folded, a pose that was fast becoming disturbingly familiar.

Her smile faded as his intentions finally sank in. He expected her to stay here—alone—with him. "No," she said firmly, even though he hadn't asked the question yet.

His dark head tilted. "Those are my conditions. You stay here and work on the diamond in the room provided until the job is done."

Frowning, she shook her head slowly.

"It's not negotiable."

Dani thought he sounded bored. "I'm not staying here alone with you."

His eyes were scathing. "Don't be puerile, Ms. Hammond. Just what do you think is going to happen?"

If his intention was to make her feel gauche and stupid, it worked. "Wh-what possible reason...?" she stammered, her cheeks burning.

"Security and expediency. It is an extremely valuable diamond and I am a busy man. I don't have time to sit around up here in Nowhere-ville for a minute longer than necessary."

Dani shook her head again. "No deal. Bring the stone to the shop. I'll work on it between customers."

Quinn's brows raised. "I don't think so," he said softly, and, turning, left the room. But the certainty of his voice, his potent male presence remained.

Dani waited a couple of seconds, worried. There was sympathy in his face as he'd turned away. Her refusal had not even registered. A vision of being locked in, of pushing against him, pounding against his broad chest to get out, made her head swim.

She was being ridiculous. Quinn Everard was an internationally regarded man in the gem and fine arts world. He was not going to kidnap her. She started off after him. "Look, if you're worried about theft, don't be. There hasn't been a robbery in town for years."

"You don't understand, Ms. Hammond." He turned so sharply to face her that she almost bumped into his impressive chest. "This is a very special diamond."

"It will be perfectly safe in the shop, and, anyway, I'm insured."

His eyes bored into her, making her heart thump. She stepped back hurriedly, excruciatingly aware that he hadn't given an inch.

"Have you heard of the Distinction Diamond, Danielle?"

"The Dist...?" Air punched out from her lungs and her heart thudded. Either that or her chin hit the floor. The Distinction Diamond was nearly forty carats of fancy intense yellow, originating from the Kimberley mines in South Africa. No one had heard of it for years. "You've got the Distinction Diamond?" Her swallow was audible. "Here?"

Quinn Everard could do scathing very well. Was it the curve of his lips or the dangerous glint that lit up his eyes? "No, Ms. Hammond." He turned his back and continued on to the door next to "her" room. "I have her big sister."

Two

Quinn turned his back and walked into his bedroom, smiling when he felt her creeping presence at the door. Opening the panel in the wall that concealed the safe, he began keying the code into a digital keypad. The whole house was burglar and smoke alarmed, including this room and the workroom. The safe was dual combination and key, complete with trembler sensor. His company had the best security money could buy. After all, it was vital in his business.

He glanced to where she fidgeted at the door, chewing on her bottom lip. Quinn miskeyed and the thing beeped at him. He swore softly, ordering himself to stop thinking about whiskey eyes and plump bottom lips. She was on the hook. It was time to reel her in.

He went through the elaborate security measures

with exaggerated care, then took out a heavy steel box from which he lifted a hand-stitched leather case after a barrage of additional code numbers. A hydraulic mechanism raised a small velvet-covered platform on which the diamond sat. Reaching out, he flicked the desk lamp on. Then he faced her and tilted his head, giving her permission to come near.

She moved slowly into the room, her eyes on his face. The light from the lamp washed over her skin, and he thought again, as he had earlier on meeting her, that her face was all wrong, a contradiction. Wide-set, wild-honey eyes, a straight no-nonsense nose, and then rosebud lips, suggesting innocence and insecurity.

And just like earlier when he'd first looked at her, the impact jolted him. She'd attempted to tame her wildfire hair with a scarf, but still, dark red curls sprang up in interesting dimensions. Her colour sense was outrageous, combining a red-and-pink-striped top with a captivatingly short floral skirt. She was exotic, unconventional, bubbling over with life and energy. He knew more beautiful women, but none so colourful, so vibrantly original.

She looked down at the diamond on display for her, her eyes glowing. When she finally looked back at Quinn, the gratitude in her eyes stunned him. She would know well how few people had ever been given the opportunity to look upon this treasure.

Enjoy it, he thought grimly. If it were down to him, he wouldn't have Danielle Hammond within one hundred metres of this baby, no matter how interesting her face.

She put out her hand. It hovered over the glow and she hesitated. "May I?"

Half of him wondered what the diamond would look like against her skin, her hair. The other half protested, *Get the hell away from this diamond!* But he had his orders. He nodded tersely.

Her slim hand dipped and the middle finger stroked lightly, reverently over the crown of the perfect octahedron. Then she took her hands away, crossed them in front of her body and just looked down at the stone, as if giving thanks to a god. Her lashes made shadows on her cheek.

"Do we have a deal, Ms. Hammond?" he asked quietly, reluctant to interrupt what was obviously an awe-inspiring moment for her. As it had been for him when he had procured this very special diamond for his client six years ago.

"I have a choice?" she murmured.

He knew she didn't. No jeweller in her right mind would say no to this opportunity.

She continued, "Since you're blackmailing me…"

Quinn smiled at her nice recovery. "Of course I am." He knew that she would crawl over broken glass to get her hands on this stone, blackmail or not. Money or not.

He perched on the edge of the desk. "The conditions are these—you stay here in the house for the duration of the work. You work on it day and night if possible. You tell no one about this stone."

She sucked in a breath. "I have a life, you know."

"No, you don't." He shook his head decisively. "Not for the next few weeks."

"And my shop?"

Quinn had initiated a decent conversation with the

young hippie called Steve in her little shop this morning. "Your assistant needs more hours. His partner is pregnant. They're struggling financially."

Dani frowned. "You found all that out in a couple of minutes?"

"I did not draw your name out of a hat, Ms. Hammond," he said sharply. While he couldn't blame her for being surprised, his reputation alone should have swayed her. Put that together with one of the most incredible stones the world had ever seen and it was unfathomable that he was still trying to persuade her.

"What sort of setting?"

Quinn shrugged. "You're the designer."

"I mean," she sighed, "pendant? Brooch? What type of piece? I didn't see any cutting gear."

He drew himself up to full height. "You will not touch this stone with anything but your fingers, do you hear?"

Danielle Hammond rolled her eyes at him. "Of course not, but I may use other gems." She eyed him speculatively. "You are supplying findings? Platinum, diamonds, the whole deal?"

"As long as you keep the stone whole, you have carte blanche to design whatever you like. I will need to approve a model and a list of your requirements."

"This could take weeks…."

"You have three, less is preferable. The accommodation is acceptable?"

She nodded.

"I will feed you. Everything you need for the job is there. All you need to do is tap into your talent and work."

"Who's it for?"

Quinn opened his mouth, staring at her face. "A friend," he said shortly. "A special friend."

Dani nodded, and he could almost hear her mind ticking over. That was his brief; she was not to know who commissioned the piece. No harm letting her think there was a special lady friend. "Do we have a deal?"

She exhaled noisily and stared down at the diamond as if for reassurance.

Just to play with her longing, he closed the lid—slowly.

"I want half the money up front," she said, "and throw in Steve's wages."

He scowled. "How very Blackstone of you." Her family connections were his main objection to the deal. Quinn had no time for anyone bearing the Blackstone stamp and was sorely tempted to delegate this job to one of his staff. But it was a sensitive matter, one which he'd reluctantly agreed to handle personally.

He picked the box up off the desk, noting with pleasure the regret and loss in her eyes as she watched him put it away.

"This is going to be a barrel of laughs," Dani muttered from behind his back.

"The sooner you get on with it, the quicker we can go our separate ways." He banged the safe door closed. "I'll take you home to pack and make arrangements."

When he turned back to her, she was rubbing the side of her long pale neck, eyes closed, her head rolled back. Quinn teetered on the edge of a rogue wave of desire so intense that it stopped him dead in his tracks. Behind her, not two feet away, his king-size bed sprawled, inspiring all sorts of suggestive images.

Her eyes snapped open, finding his gaze immediately. "No need. My place is only a minute or two from here."

He gestured to the door. "I'll drive you," he said firmly, intent on getting her out of his bedroom.

Quinn prowled her living room while she packed and made arrangements to cover her absence from her shop. He was fond of his comforts, and the climate up here in Northern Queensland was not to his liking. Luckily, unlike Dani's tiny apartment in a dated resort complex, the beach house was equipped with an excellent air-conditioning system. He wiped the back of his neck while she scurried about packing with the phone plastered to her ear. The prospect of baby-sitting a spoiled girl with an artistic temperament and inflated opinion of her own talent, whilst sweltering in the suffocating humidity, was not a good one.

His internal temperature soared even higher when later that afternoon, after settling in at his rental, his house guest took a swim. Quinn's office window offered an unobstructed view of the pool. His work forgotten, he stood at the window, watching the long-legged, flame-haired beauty. She wore long shorts and an oversize T-shirt; perfectly respectable attire—until it got wet. Quinn turned the air-conditioning dial down a couple of notches and undid the top two buttons of his shirt.

For the first time in many years, he wanted, with a savage unrelenting intensity. He was certainly not celibate, but preferred older, cultured and financially independent women. Women with similar interests and social mores as he. Danielle Hammond looked to be mid-to-late twenties and certainly had the wealth of the Blackstones behind her, but they were light-years apart.

It was totally undignified to stand at a window, salivating over the sights of wet fabric clinging lovingly to a fine pair of breasts, and of water streaming down well-toned, lightly tanned legs. He was much too discriminating to crave the slide of her wet, spiralling curls on his burning skin. Wasn't he?

He returned to his desk, pushing aside the unwelcome intrusion. This wasn't supposed to be a holiday, he chided himself. The next Famous Paintings auction was only days away. It was frustrating to be stuck here for such an important date on his professional calendar, but at least he had a contact to inspect a very special lot number for one of his most important clients.

Clearing his head one final time, he refocussed his attention where it belonged. On his work. He remained at his desk until Danielle interrupted him, after the dinner hour. Apparently she was ready to work and wanted the diamond to be brought to the workroom.

Quinn set it up on the workbench and watched her circle the desk, her small digital camera clicking and whirring as she took snapshot after snapshot.

He was totally absorbed by her concentration, not to mention her lithe form bending and stretching, and the interesting strain of fabric across her rump and thighs as she crouched and circled. So when she suddenly straightened and looked at him, he was a few seconds behind the eight ball.

Her finely arched brows seemed to mock him. "What's she like?"

"I beg your pardon?"

"Your lady friend. The one you're giving the diamond to."

"Like?"

She looked at the ceiling briefly. "Her height and build. I don't want to design something dainty for a big strapping girl. Or vice versa."

Quinn hesitated. It wasn't an unreasonable request.

Tonight she wore flowing baggy summer pants of an indeterminate colour that fell between pewter and light brown. A purple lacy top accentuated her shape, which was, he conceded, a work of art. A strip of matching fabric tied bandanna-style kept her forehead free of springy curls, and lime-green beads circled her throat. "Five nine, five ten." He shrugged. "Slender but strong-looking."

Dani held the camera up, checking the images. Quinn noted with surprise that her nails were short and some of them jagged, as if she chewed them.

"Pale or tan?" she asked distractedly.

"Lightly tanned," he told her. "Freckles."

Click, click. "Okay. Hair?" When he didn't answer immediately, she lowered the camera and frowned at him. "What colour is her hair?"

Several superlative responses came to mind, but while he was deciding which best described her vibrant curls, her frown gave way to sarcasm. "You're a little unobservant, Mr. Everard. Do you have a photo, perhaps?"

His mouth quirked. "Red. Dark red." He pursed his lips, wondering when she would twig. "Curly."

Her brows arched up to kiss the edge of the bandanna.

"Rather multifaceted in style," Quinn went on, warming to his task. "Unconventional, definitely. Some would say bohemian, but that's not it… She's like no one else." And that was the truth. Her use of colour, breaking all the fashion rules, should have offended a conservative like himself, yet somehow, it charmed the hell out of him. Living with Danielle Hammond, he knew, would never be boring.

Dani pursed her lips sternly. "You have good taste in women, Mr. Everard," she told him smartly, and put the camera down with a sharp thud. "Contemporary bling, then, for the lady."

"Knock yourself out." Quinn pushed himself away from the doorjamb, trying not to be horrified about her terminology in reference to this diamond. He'd spent hours trying to talk his client out of this, citing Danielle's age and inexperience.

Surprisingly though, he smiled all the way down the hall, pleased with himself, and with her. Maybe the next few weeks wouldn't be so bad, after all. Dani Hammond had a bite to her. She seemed smart—almost street-smart—and Quinn knew all about that.

But how did she, with her luxurious upbringing?

Sightings of Dani were scarce the next couple of days as she immersed herself in her design. She worked late and rose late. Mid-morning she would request he bring the diamond to the workroom. He restored it to the safe on his way to bed. He kept the refrigerator stocked and was thankfully spared the ignominy of standing by the window like a Peeping Tom, because she didn't use the pool again. Most of the food he prepared went to waste as she said she was too busy to be hungry. Despite himself, and without seeing any tangible results yet, he was impressed by her dedication.

The third night, she joined him for dinner, an impressive meal catered by one of Port Douglas's surprisingly fine restaurants.

"Why me?" she asked over coffee. "You must know twenty world-class designers who would gnaw off their right hand to ingratiate themselves with you."

He tapped his teaspoon lightly on the cup, giving a brief smile. "But not you."

"Aren't you afraid I'll mess up your precious diamond out of spite since you're blackmailing me?"

"Then I would have to mess up your reputation."

"Haven't you already?" She raised and crooked her two index fingers in a parody of speech marks. "'Ms. Hammond has passable talent but chooses to use it working for chain stores....'"

Quinn rubbed his ear, amused. That was one of his missives in the *DiamondWorld Monthly* about a year ago. She'd had the cheek to respond in the next issue. He'd retaliated by saying she was "one step up from a Sunday-market vendor in a one-horse town, pandering to the tourist buses."

"A mere dent, which doesn't seem to have harmed

you at all. Although, why you would shut yourself away up here in the middle of nowhere is anyone's guess."

"Another snobby Sydney-sider," she sighed, giving him the impression this wasn't the first time she'd had this conversation. "I like the tropics."

"What's to like? A beach you can't swim in because of the stingers…"

"Only for a few months…"

"Insufferably hot and sticky weather…"

"I like it probably for all the reasons you don't. Especially now in cyclone season."

So the lady was into sultry, steamy nights. He sniffed and rubbed his jaw, clamping down on where that thought would take him. "Bugs and snakes…"

"You get those in Sydney," she countered.

"Not in *my* neighbourhood, you don't."

"They wouldn't dare," she muttered under her breath.

He ignored that. "No shopping to speak of. Is there actually any nightlife in town or does it shut down at five-thirty?"

"Remind me to take you cane toad racing while you're here," she said, then smiled wryly and leaned her elbows on the table edge. "Laid-back it might be, but there's an interesting dynamic of village charm and sophistication here. Port is famous for its restaurants and you never know which Hollywood stars or ex-American president you'll bump into around town or checking out the reef in their big chartered yachts."

His fingers tapped the tabletop, drawing her glance. "We know you like to play with the rich and famous, but you're limiting your opportunities here, Danielle. Why is that?"

"I do all right, and don't call me Danielle."

He inclined his head. "And 'all right' is enough?"

"For now." She sipped her coffee. "Tell me about you and Howard."

"You don't know?" he asked, surprised.

Dani shook her head. "I was at uni around that time. All I know is, he bristled every time your name came up."

That didn't surprise him. Back then, Howard Blackstone had thrown his whole vindictive weight against the young broker from the wrong side of the tracks. "I was just starting out," he began. Laura, his wife, was sick. His whole world was going to hell.

"Howard wanted to be nominated as the Australian representative to the new World Association of Diamonds. Everyone had finally woken up to the fact that our industry, the diamond trade, was subsidising wars in Africa."

"Conflict diamonds." Dani nodded. "What good could some worldwide association do against the one or two massive conglomerates who control the mines?"

Sharp, he thought, but then she had grown up in Australia's foremost mining family. "The association has definitely raised awareness. Even America, the largest bastion of consumerism, reports that a high percentage of people in the market ask for certification that their diamond is conflict-free."

"A certificate's only as good as the person who completes it," she stated, again rousing grudging admiration for her appraisal of a very grey area.

"So, the feud?" Dani prompted.

Quinn pushed his empty plate aside and leaned back. "Blackstone wined and dined me. He wanted my vote. I suppose he could have got the impression I was a solid bet, but in the end, a fellow broker asked and my vote went his way. To be honest, I expected Howard to romp in, with or without me."

"But he didn't." Dani nodded. "He likes—liked—getting his own way."

Quinn wondered about the relationship between her and Australia's King of Diamonds. "He lost the nomination by one vote, and took it a lot more personally than it warranted."

"Let me guess. You were off the Christmas card list."

Well and truly, Quinn thought grimly. Howard's wrath nearly sent him to the wall with his financiers. "He banned me from accessing the Blackstone mines. I had to borrow heavily to source the stones I needed offshore."

If it hadn't been for one or two friends in high places—notably Sir John Knowles, owner of the diamond upstairs—Quinn's fledgling business wouldn't have survived.

Dani whistled. "That must have hurt. The broker with no diamonds."

"It put me in a very bad situation," he agreed.

She glanced around the room, her eyes resting on a magenta orchid in the corner. "It doesn't seem to have had any long-term consequences."

"No thanks to the Blackstones."

"Have you approached Ric or Ryan? They may be willing to ease the ban now."

Now that Howard was dead, Quinn thought scathingly. His dislike of the former head of Blackstone Diamonds wasn't just business. Howard had made it personal. How ironic that he was sitting across an elegant table with his nemesis's protégée. "I can manage without the precious Blackstone mines, thanks."

Dani's gaze sharpened a little. "Forgive and forget, hey? The man's dead."

He couldn't forget. The slights in the papers. Door after door closing in his face. The old-boys banking networks, determined to pull him down. "It's hard enough starting out without the most influential man in the business doing a number on you."

And all while he was barely keeping his head above water to cope with his wife's terminal illness.

And that's where Howard's vindictiveness really came into its own. Quinn could overlook the loss of business, the tearing down of his reputation, the condescending snubs by former backers. He would never forgive the look in Laura's eyes when he couldn't give her the one thing she wanted above all else.

It never failed to surprise him how much it grated after all these years. "Howard Blackstone was a manipulative, vindictive bastard."

Dani blanched, and just for a moment, he felt a needle of sympathy. Was it possible that someone in this world mourned the man so many hated?

"You know all about being vindictive, don't you?" she asked tightly. "Wasn't that what marking me down at the awards was about? Or the slagging off you gave me in various industry papers?" She drained her cup and banged it down on the saucer. "Maybe you and Howard aren't so different after all."

"Maybe you just aren't that good," he suggested, eying her evenly.

"If that's so," she snapped, "why am I here?"

"I don't know, *Danielle*." He stressed the syllables of her name. "Haven't you got work to do?"

She glared, and in the candlelight, her hair and eyes crackled like embers. "Luckily, it's a big house, Mr. Everard. Why don't we keep our distance?"

She shoved herself to her feet and stalked from the room.

Three

"Fine by me!"

Dani slammed the door on his retort and stomped up the stairs, muttering to herself.

Granted, Howard Blackstone had been no angel. His abrasive nature combined with immense wealth was the perfect enemy magnet, but that aside, he had provided a good life for her and her mother. Sonya and Dani Hammond were two of the very few people in this world who truly mourned him.

She opened the workroom door and banged that, too. Bloody man!

Sonya had moved in with Howard and her sister, Ursula, when she was twelve years old. After their first-born was abducted, Ursula became depressed and took her own life. Howard was inconsolable so Sonya stayed on to look after her niece Kimberley and nephew Ryan. When she became pregnant, Howard persuaded her to remain and bring up her child with all the advantages his own children enjoyed. He paid for Dani's education, and over the years, they'd forged quite an affectionate bond. Sometimes she thought he liked her better than he did his own children.

Her mother had refuted that. "He loves Kim and Ryan fiercely. He enjoys your company because he has hopes for you rather than expectations of you."

People didn't know the real Howard, Dani thought belligerently, tearing off her latest mishmash of a sketch. His faults were legion, but she and Sonya saw a side of him he didn't show to many. They would always be grateful.

By unspoken mutual consent, Dani and Quinn avoided each other the next day. She needed to pinpoint a design, but every time she looked at the diamond, her ideas changed. She held it up to the light, admiring the purity, depth and distribution of colour throughout. There was a cynical old saying popular in her trade: a polished diamond is only rough ruined. How she wished to have seen this beauty before it was cut.

Dozens of pages littered the floor under the sketch pad as she pared back the initial outpouring of inspiration into a few shapes vaguely resembling a setting she might be able to work with. About the only thing she knew for sure was that the setting would be platinum because it complemented a diamond's finest qualities so perfectly, especially fancy pinks and yellows. Dani intended the stone to be the star, not the setting.

As the hours passed, ideas rushed through her mind, most disappearing a few seconds after their arrival. She played around on the software Quinn had provided, but the solution eluded her and the beautiful diamond taunted her on its velvet pillow. Finally she took it from the display box and slid down to the floor with it in her hand, loving the milky coolness of it in her palm.

Quinn walked into the room with a plate in one hand and utensils and a wineglass in the other. He stared at her incredulously for a moment, then turned to set his load on the desk. Dani pressed back against the leg of the workbench, suddenly wondering what her hair looked like. Had she showered today or not…?

She gazed at him, thinking how seriously appealing he was. He wore pleated charcoal chinos and a light polo shirt that accentuated the breadth of his shoulders and had her peeking at his strongly muscled arms. Boat shoes, no socks. His platinum Rolex flashed as he leaned forward to switch a lamp on.

"What are you doing?" he asked, staring down at her sternly.

"Thinking. What's it look like?"

After a pause, he nodded at the food he'd brought. "Eat."

"What time is it?" She raised her head to peer out the window. It was dark. Where had the day gone?

"Eight." He frowned at the sight of the uneaten sub he had brought up at lunch, the cold cup of coffee beside it.

Still holding the diamond, she uncrossed her legs and rose, drawn by the smell of the food. A twinge in her stomach reminded her she'd had little to eat today, if anything. She replaced the diamond in its box and reached for the wineglass first.

"How's it going?"

The wine was smooth. She swallowed and opened her mouth to answer but was hijacked by a huge yawn. "'Kay."

It wasn't okay yet, it was driving her nuts. Inspiration never came easy. She could spend hours or even days on an idea and toss it because of a niggling suspicion she had seen it somewhere. Originality was paramount.

His large shoe ventured out to drag a ball of screwed-up paper toward him. "What time did you work till last night?"

She shrugged, still smouldering a little from their altercation the night before. It would be better if he'd just leave her alone with her thoughts and her food.

"Eating and sleeping will be tolerated on an occasional basis."

Had he made a joke? Emboldened, she moved closer to the food he'd brought, suddenly ravenous. "Thanks." The wine had cleansed her palate and spiced her appetite, and she sniffed appreciatively.

"Is there a problem with your setting?" He bent to pick up the ball of paper by his shoe.

"No." Dani picked up the fork and stabbed at a floret of bright green broccoli. "I haven't nailed it yet, but don't worry. I will."

Quinn tossed the ball of paper into the trash bin. Then he moved to the easel and tilted his head at the latest sketch, one she hadn't torn off yet. "Have the graphics I supplied been any help?"

Dani shook her head and cut into tender lamb drizzled with a sauce that tasted of paprika. Software was great for learning on, but most designers she knew preferred to work freestyle.

He moved to the desk where she sat and laid his hand on her portfolio. "May I?"

Dani stilled mid-chew. His past comments about her work still rankled. Yet here she was, staying in luxury accommodations, being catered for to her heart's desire. Awaiting the payment of a colossal sum of money, and all for the privilege of working on an incredible diamond.

She shrugged. Whatever he thought of her stuff, he'd paid her an enormous compliment by commissioning her. Quinn Everard, the great Australian gem expert, wanted *her* to design for him. Not Cartier. Not JAR. Dani Hammond.

Quinn flicked the desk lamp on and stood, one hand in his pocket, the other leisurely turning the pages of the big black binder. He studied each page intently, unmoving except for his lashes dipping and rising as his eyes moved over the page. She watched under the guise of chewing and swallowing.

His shirt clung to the contours of his chest and hinted at an impressive-looking abdominal ridge or two. Fine dark hair sprinkled his forearms. The harsh light of the lamp picked out definite traces of silver in his sideburns. Mid-thirties, she guessed, with plenty of exercise to keep him toned and strong.

She tore her eyes away before he caught her, suddenly feeling way too warm. Quinn was too big for this room, too enticing and wickedly attractive.

His deep brown eyes were suddenly on her face. "These are good."

She hadn't realised she was holding her breath, but now it suddenly left her in a rush. "Oh. Thanks."

"You have improved, matured."

Improved? Matured? *Don't go overboard with the compliments, mate.* "Thanks," she sniffed, and turned back to her nearly empty plate.

"Maybe," he continued, "you chose the wrong piece for the awards."

"You were the only one who thought so."

That was a lie. She had thought that, worried about it. Her entry for the Young Designer Awards was a wide gold bangle featuring pink and white Blackstone diamonds. It was supposed to capture the sweep of the outback ranges and show the riches within. Although it was a stunning piece and created comment from whoever saw it, Dani had never felt peaceful about it, never felt that she actually got it.

Quinn Everard, the judge, was the only one who had seen past the "wow" factor and found it wanting.

"Now, this…"

He flipped the pages back to where his thumb had marked the spot. She stood up and moved beside him, inhaling a warm masculinity so clean and refreshing that the air in the room was revitalised. Dani nearly swayed with the pleasure of being close to him, her fatigue from the long day washing away.

She looked down at the book. "The Keishi!" This was one of her first pieces, and still a favourite. Nineteen millimetre champagne Keishi pearls strung on white gold interspersed with gold roses, each centre a small round blue sapphire.

"This would have won you the award, just for colour and lustre alone."

She thrummed with pleasure. "I wanted to enter it. People said it wasn't high value enough."

Quinn looked into her eyes and her heartbeat stuttered.

Heat bloomed inside and filled her. She couldn't look away for the life of her. This close she picked out the fine lines at the corner of his eyes; the scar by his mouth she wanted to trace with her finger to see if it was as smooth as it looked. His eyes were dark and a little perplexed, and then he looked down at her mouth.

"Trust your instincts," he said softly.

Oh, boy, if he only knew what her instincts were telling her now. He was so close, his breath wafted over her face. She felt her body tighten, sway slightly in his direction. The man was a magnet, her own personalised magnet. The back of her neck prickled and dampened under the rumpled hank of hair she had twisted and last looked at ten hours ago.

Ten hours ago? She stepped back hurriedly, thinking how dishevelled she must look. There was probably broccoli in her teeth, and she remembered now that she had not showered today....

Dani had her pride. She didn't even know if she liked this man, but if succumbing to an intense attraction was an option, she would at least be clean and fragrant.

"I—I think it's time for bed." She groaned inwardly, thinking, *You smooth talker, you.* Her embarrassment was heightened by how strangely husky her voice sounded.

"It's only eight."

She ran her tongue over her teeth. "It's been a long day."

Quinn nodded, and in the process, his eyes swept over her chest and lingered long enough to tell her what she already knew, that her nipples were tight and hard, visibly so.

She didn't dare look down. "You can take the diamond to bed," she said weakly, then wanted to clap her hands to her head. Verbal clumsiness didn't sneak up on her often, but she'd made the world team tonight.

Quinn's mouth twitched.

Her cheeks stung with heat. No doubt his "lady friend" would be so much more sophisticated, never a hair out of place or a word out of turn.

"You look hot, Dani," Quinn said smoothly, and there was no mistaking his amusement.

She cleared her throat. "You could check the air-con in here. These lights really raise the temperature."

"They do, don't they?"

She'd made enough of a fool of herself. "Good night." She escaped without waiting for his response.

Quinn let his head roll back and stared at the bright lights on the ceiling. "Control yourself," he muttered, his weakness taunting him. Had she noticed his arousal? He'd sure noticed hers! The sexual charge he got just from being in the same room was beyond a joke, and he was toast once he clapped eyes on her chest.

So despite her snippiness, the lady was interested.

That added a new dimension to the proceedings. He'd not so much as touched her, but he knew instinctively that they were sexually compatible, or more aptly, explosively combustible!

Interesting… He looked down at her empty plate, remembering why he'd come up here in the first place. Quinn was tired of his own company, bored eating alone—which was weird since he was used to it. Preferred it, in fact. His life was a never-ending roundabout of fancy dinners in up-market restaurants, with the added non-bonus of countless airline meals.

But his apartment in Sydney was ordered and peaceful. To his mind, a cheese sandwich in front of the wall-to-ceiling windows that showcased the most beautiful city in the world was far more enjoyable than any two-hundred-dollar meal he had ever eaten.

A throwback, he supposed, to the chaotic mealtimes at home when he was a kid.

Quinn grew up with loving but eccentric parents who filled their huge old Sydney home to overflowing with troubled foster kids. He shared everything as a boy: his parents' love and time, his room, toys, even his wife, who moved in while they were at university. She was studying to be a social worker and loved helping out with the kids. Quinn shared her right up to the day she died of a brain tumour, aged twenty-six.

These days, he didn't share so much anymore, but still loved his parents dearly. Although he wished they didn't keep asking him when he was going to get around to giving them grandkids. Quinn's response hadn't changed since he was twenty: "I learned growing up that there are too many unwanted kids in the world."

He picked up the boxed diamond and took it to his room to lock away. Then he collected her empty plate and the food he'd brought at lunch. His phone rang as he descended the stairs. Matt Hammond calling from New Zealand.

He'd met Matt before since they were both shareholders of several different companies, including Blackstone Diamonds.

"Can we meet up in the next week?" Matt asked. "Among other things, I'd like to thank you properly for bringing the pink diamonds home."

Last month, Quinn had authenticated four pink diamonds for Matt's former sister-in-law, Melbourne supermodel, Briana Davenport. Briana found them in her apartment safe after her sister Marise was killed in the plane crash. Quinn was astonished to find they were from the Blackstone Rose necklace, stolen from Howard nearly three decades ago. He told Briana they must be returned to their rightful owner. At her request, he'd delivered the stones to Howard Blackstone's estate lawyers.

It was well publicised that Howard's will had been altered shortly before the crash to bestow his jewellery collection to Marise. Quinn was less clear on whether the stolen necklace would be included in the jewellery collection, since it was not specifically named and still listed as stolen. He had to be sure he was not acting illegally. It would pan out better for Briana, his client, that way.

After deliberation, the lawyers declared that the Blackstone Rose necklace *was* included in the jewellery collection. Since Marise hadn't changed her will before the accident, the pink diamonds now belonged to her spouse, Matt Hammond.

"I'm holidaying in Port Douglas for the next couple of weeks," Quinn told Matt now.

"You're kidding! I'm coming up there myself in the next couple of days. We can catch up then, if you're agreeable."

Quinn wondered if Matt was coming to Port Douglas to see Dani. They were cousins, but from what he'd heard, the rift between the Blackstones and the Hammonds included both Dani and her mother, Sonya.

"In the meantime," Matt continued, "I'd like you to put the word out. I'm willing to ask no questions and pay top dollar for the fifth Blackstone Rose diamond, the big one."

The centrepiece of the old necklace was a pear-shaped 9.7 carat diamond. The original Heart of the Outback stone was just over one hundred carats in the rough. Stones lost a lot of weight in the cutting, especially if the cutter wanted several diamonds from the one stone. Some cutters went for weight, which did not necessarily correlate to value; fire and brilliance came from the shape the cutter chose.

In this case, the cutter had done a masterful job, re-alising a creditable thirty-eight carats in total. This, along with the name and the legend, accorded the stones a massive price tag. The last big intense pink Quinn could recall coming up for auction several years ago—an unnamed twenty carat, pear-shaped beauty—fetched six million dollars. The Blackstone Rose diamonds could sell for as much as half a million dollars per carat, more if they were sold together.

Although laser identification wasn't around when the stones were cut, the Blackstone Rose's thief must have sold the big stone on the black market for it to have disappeared without a trace. Quinn had extensive connections, and there was always someone who could be persuaded to sell information about less-reputable art and gem collectors. A pink of this size would cause comment wherever it turned up.

Quinn hung up, thinking that his whole existence lately—professional and personal—seemed to be tied up with the Blackstone and Hammond families. First Matt and the pink diamonds, now his enforced cohabitation with Danielle Hammond. His very *personal* existence stirred again when he recalled the desire in her eyes a few minutes ago, heard the huskiness of her voice. He knew that he was destined to spend another night alone in his bed, dreaming about her intriguing face and lithe body.

He would have Dani Hammond, he decided. It would help while away the hours in this sauna until he could return to civilisation.

He grinned as he stripped and slid between the sheets, allowing himself the uncharitable thought that tupping Howard Blackstone's little girl would be like thumbing his nose at the old man, dead or not. That would be twice in a month he'd shafted the old goat. Howard must have turned in his freshly dug grave when the Blackstone Rose diamonds came full circle to a Hammond again.

Four

Soon after 6:00 a.m., an ungodly time for her, Dani crept out of the house to watch the sun rise over the beach. The tide was high and the temperature around twenty. Yawning widely, she stumbled through the ten-metre stretch of trees that fringed the beach, then slipped off her sandals and carried them down to test the water.

The physical response she'd had to Quinn in the workroom had played on her mind all night. Her fumbling efforts to gloss over it, knowing he'd noticed her tongue practically hanging out, made it ten times worse.

This man was not her friend. More than that, he already had a woman, a special woman, judging by the value of the gift he was having made for her. But why did he have to be so gorgeous? How was she to exist under the same roof for the next two to three weeks without succumbing to his charms?

She knew how. Remember Nick…remember the humiliation.

The water licked around her toes, a cool surprise, reminding her that winter was on its way. She remembered a cool winter's day two years ago. On cue, her cheeks burned for no one but her and the breeze as she walked on deserted Four Mile Beach. Nick had nearly finished her.

Dani should have known better, even back then. Twenty-five was hardly wet behind the ears. Nick had wined and dined her, swept her off her feet in an indecently short time. Promised love and marriage and forever. And even though she'd lived all her life in a fishbowl being targeted by the Sydney tabloids, she trusted him.

Until the day she'd left the house to go to a wedding dress fitting and found ten journalists camped outside the gate in the rain. To this day, Dani loathed large black umbrellas. They reminded her of vultures waiting for someone to die.

The journalists gleefully filled her in on the details. While she'd been sitting at home happily planning her wedding, Nick had been entertaining a well-known soap actress in an alleyway beside a nightclub. The photographs were pornographic. When confronted, the louse drunkenly accused Dani of misrepresenting her position in the Blackstone family. It had finally sunk in, despite her repeated insistence, that far from being an heiress, his fiancée was penniless and illegitimate.

Howard came to her rescue, just as he had for her mother years before. Dani wanted nothing more than to disappear. A few months backpacking around Asia eased her pain a little but caused her mother tremendous worry. Tired of the constant media scrutiny, she refused to return to Sydney, and Howard agreed to bankroll her business here in Port, where no one knew or cared that she was Danielle Hammond of Blackstone fame.

The sunrise was beautiful, reminding her of why she loved this place. She filled her lungs with sea air, knowing she had to resist Quinn, because if she didn't, there would be far worse heartache than Nick had inflicted. And that would spoil this beautiful place for her forever.

She turned around at the halfway point, feeling stronger and determined to finish this job quickly and eliminate the temptation. But her heart fluttered as a figure in blue shorts and a black sleeveless T-shirt jogged leisurely toward her. She had forgotten he liked to run in the early morning before the heat and humidity gained purchase.

Quinn slowed as she approached. "Too hot to sleep?"

Whether it was there or not, Dani imagined a sardonic twist to his mouth, and her hope that he would ignore her stammering reaction to him last night faded. He knew. And he wanted her to know he knew.

"Have a good run," she said as politely as she could muster, still walking steadily toward the turnoff through the trees.

But Quinn began jogging backward, facing her. "Did you know Matt Hammond is coming to town?"

That was unexpected. She slowed. "No, I didn't."

Dani had never met Matt in person. He'd attended Howard's funeral in February but kept an icy distance from the family. She'd wanted to introduce herself but decided, under the circumstances, to present a united front with the family of the man who had raised her.

She'd met Matt's brother Jarrod a couple of times and liked him immensely. But Matt was understandably bitter about Marise's presence on the ill-fated plane and her inclusion in the diamond magnate's will. Especially when a lot of the bad press zeroed in on the paternity of little Blake, Matt and Marise's son.

"How did you know that?" Dani asked.

"He called last night."

"Called you?" She frowned.

Quinn stopped jogging and propped his foot on a half-buried log to retie his laces. "We're both in the gem trade. That's not so odd, is it?"

Dani hovered nearby, curious.

"When I told him where I was, he said he was on his way here himself. I assumed, since you're his cousin, it was to see you."

She shook her head. "He wouldn't come here to see me."

Quinn utilised the log to stretch his calf muscles. Dani couldn't help but notice the dark hair salting his long strong legs.

She wrenched her mind back to Matt. Why would he seek her out? And what was his business with Quinn? A mutual dislike of Howard Blackstone was their only connection as far as she could see. "What exactly is your business with Matt?"

Quinn stilled, his hands on his thighs. "Is that anything to do with you?"

"Is it to do with the Blackstone Rose diamonds?"

"What do you know of the Blackstone Rose diamonds?"

Dani exhaled. "How they mysteriously turned up at Howard's lawyers a month ago and they had no choice but to send them to Hammonds." Suddenly it all fell into place. "*You* found them. *You* sent them back."

"I didn't find them. I was given them. A simple authentication job."

"Who from?"

"You'll have to ask Matt for the details, but they're his property, fair and square."

"I told you, I don't know him." She sighed. "He came to the funeral but wouldn't have anything to do with us."

"You should be more picky whom you fraternise with," Quinn said lightly. "Is there anyone in the world Howard Blackstone hasn't rubbed up the wrong way?"

"The feud wasn't all Howard's doing, you know."

"Tell me about it."

"Everyone knows. You must know."

"I know what the papers say." Quinn sat down on the log and patted the space beside him. "I want to hear it from an insider."

She sat tautly, aware of his big hot body just inches away, warming her side. A trickle of sweat crawled down his temple and she bet his back would be slick, too. Why didn't that turn her right off, instead of accelerating her pulse to alarming levels?

She bent and picked up a handful of white sand, letting it run slowly through her fingers. Since Howard's death, the Blackstone-Hammond feud origins had been printed and reprinted. Dani was sorry if her rendition was reminiscent of a bored teenage boy recounting his summer holiday to his class, but frankly, she was tired of the whole thing.

"Jeb, my granddad, and Howard were friends and partners after Howard married my auntie Ursula. Uncle Oliver, Mum and Ursula's brother, was left behind in New Zealand to run the family business. Anyway, when Granddad Jeb got sick, he signed over all his mining claims to Howard. Naturally, this didn't go down too well with Oliver."

That was an understatement. According to her cousin Jarrod, even after a stroke five years ago, the old man still got apoplectic at the mere mention of Howard Blackstone.

"He was particularly upset when Jeb gifted the Heart of the Outback stone, his most famous find, to Auntie Ursula." The massive pink diamond was part of Australian folklore, but as with many other exceptional diamonds, it brought its own share of bad luck with it.

"Howard had it cut and set into a fabulous necklace he called the Blackstone Rose."

"Rubbing salt into Hammond's wound," Quinn murmured.

She nodded. Oliver was incensed that the name Hammond was now completely usurped of its rightful place in the history of the famous Heart of the Outback.

"But after James, Howard's firstborn, was abducted,

Auntie Ursula became depressed. To cheer her up, Howard threw a huge thirtieth birthday party. Everyone was there, even the prime minister." Dani smiled, remembering her mother's awestruck tone as she'd described the finery, the dresses, the beautiful decorations. "But it all ended in tears."

"The night the necklace was stolen," Quinn murmured.

Everyone had their theories. Some thought it was a failed ransom attempt. No doubt Quinn thought Howard had hidden the necklace to collect the insurance money. "Howard accused Oliver and things got pretty heated," Dani continued. "Oliver denounced his sisters and said they were dead to him…." She turned to him, lowering the depth of her voice and adding some volume, "'So long as you have anything to do with a Blackstone!'" She wagged her index finger at him.

He smiled at her. Really smiled, and her insides melted.

"You missed a bit," Quinn admonished.

"What? Oh well, you obviously know about poor old Auntie Ursula toppling into the pool…."

"After drinking too much."

She put her finger to her lips. "We don't talk about it," she whispered dramatically. "In the melee, Howard accused Oliver of engineering the kidnapping of wee James, as well." That fact was probably not as well known as the rest.

Unfortunately, that accusation was the one thing Oliver could never forgive. He and his wife, Katherine, could not have children of their own. Jarrod and Matt were adopted.

"Nice bloke," Quinn said, an edge to his voice.

"You have to remember that he'd lost a son," Dani countered. "And whatever rumours you've heard about his womanising, Mum says he really loved Auntie Ursula. It can't have been much fun watching her struggle with depression."

Quinn didn't look impressed or moved. Whatever had gone down with him and Howard must have been spectacular. She sighed. "I don't get it, Quinn. Matt has a legitimate right to be angry, especially after the past few months. But your little spat was years ago. I wonder, why do you hate his guts still, even after his death?"

"Curiosity killed the cat." His tone was cool.

It had to be more than just the diamond-association vote, Dani reasoned. Quinn was a very successful broker, one of the most prominent in the world. She refused to believe that he still held a grudge because Howard had made life a little difficult for him years ago. "You know, your dislike of Howard borders on obsession."

He cocked a cynical brow. "That so?"

"It's too personal. What did he do? Take a woman from you?"

His bark of laughter rang out, startling her.

"Professional jealousy?" she guessed.

Or maybe she was needling, trying to pick a fight. Trying to find some external conflict to justify the internal conflict of wanting him. "He beat you to the deal of a lifetime?"

Quinn's brows knitted together. "Howard Blackstone never beat me at anything."

"Or maybe you've heard the stories and decided that you are the missing Blackstone heir." She was joking, of course, even knowing it was a terrible thing to joke about.

Howard alone always had faith that his firstborn, James, would walk through the door one day. He'd never closed the investigation and must have had a strong lead just before he died, because he changed his will. The new will effectively cut Kimberley out, favouring instead his oldest son, James should he be found within six months of Howard's death.

Naturally the press enjoyed this extra twist to the ever-changing, always-enthralling saga of the Blackstone family. Several candidates had been discussed and discarded over the past months, including Jarrod Hammond, Matt's brother. You had to hand it to Howard, she thought with a spark of admiration. He sure knew how to keep the paparazzi guessing.

Just like Quinn kept her guessing, mostly about how long it would be before she gave in to an unusually severe case of the hots… Reining in her errant thoughts, she returned to the topic of the missing heir. "Let's see, you'd be about the right age, mid-thirties. And I heard somewhere that you'd grown up in a foster home."

He spread out his fingers on his thigh, snagging her gaze for a moment. Tension curled his fingertips around his muscled leg, tension that radiated toward her in a hot cloud. Dani tore her eyes away and braved a look at his face, hearing the waves just a few metres away as if they were sloshing against her ribs.

Quinn gave no sign that he agreed or disagreed, but a rising sense of incomprehensible excitement pushed the next words from her mouth. "What, did you go to him with your theory and he laughed you out of the room?"

He stilled for a long moment, then slapped one hand on the log right beside her leg and heaved to his feet, turning to loom over her. The smell of him, sweat and soap and desire, swamped her. Then his other hand slammed down on the log on her other side.

She was trapped.

His face descended quickly to within an inch of hers, so close she could almost feel the scrape of his morning beard.

"You've got it very wrong, Danielle," he said, his soft voice at odds with the dangerous blaze of warning and desire in the espresso depths of his eyes.

Her stupid joke had pushed him too far.

"I'm not the missing Blackstone brother," he murmured, his chin dipping as he inched closer. His pupils were enlarged, the centres pinpoints of fire that hypnotised and immobilised.

"Because if I was," he continued in a low murmur that made the hairs on the back of her neck leap to attention, "I wouldn't do what I'm about to do."

Dani knew what he was about to do. She saw it coming like a train wreck—and she was chained to the tracks. It was inevitable that her head tilted back and her fingernails dug in to the rough surface of the log, bracing her. The cords on her neck stretched, rigid and tight. She watched, wide-eyed, as his face and mouth crossed the last millimetre, the point of no return.

If she'd been standing, her knees would have buckled at the first taste. They stared at each other until his salty mouth with its silky tongue started teasing hers, then she felt her eyelids flutter and close. He kissed firmly, not touching her except for his mouth, yet involving her senses totally. Every kiss she'd ever experienced was just window dressing; she'd been waiting for this, the real thing. Every man she had ever kissed before was a boy, and Quinn was here to show her how a man kissed.

Where were her cautionary affirmations? Where was her regard for that unknown woman, waiting somewhere for her diamond? That woman, at least, would understand, would realise that to be kissed like this was impossible to resist.

Dani wouldn't have stopped it; he taught her that in just a few seconds. How beautiful and right it was that she sat on a log in her favourite place in the world at sunrise, and the door to perdition was open and inviting. With his tongue stroking hers, his lips commanding hers to give him more, desire pushed her to where the sunrise would claim her, consume her with pleasure.

Then he raised his head abruptly and she sagged back onto her log, gasping for breath. The young sun disappeared behind him as he straightened, and all she could think was "I've done it now."

Quinn looked down at her, his eyes a swirling brown storm of intent. "Did that feel like a cousin's kiss, Danielle?"

While she was still trying to collect coherence and dignity—and maybe some form of protest—he turned and jogged away, his strong legs pumping, his back bristling with tension.

She registered a sharp pain in the tip of her middle

finger and raised her hand to her mouth to nibble at the splinter.

She was so out of her depth.

Five

Thankfully Quinn left her alone for the rest of the day and she completed the first of several wax models she would make in these initial stages. Dani worked late, said her good-nights from his office door and went to bed, trying to dampen down the memory of the kiss. But even though she'd had little sleep the night before, it still eluded her tonight.

She tossed and turned, listening to the waves through the open window. She considered a walk along the beach, something she did sometimes when troubled or unable to sleep. But she discarded that idea, knowing all she'd see was his face, all she'd feel was his mouth on hers.

Finally at about 1:00 a.m. she rose and threw on her robe, hoping that chocolate milk might help.

Downstairs, Quinn's office light was on, the door ajar.

She halted for a minute that seemed to stretch on forever, her heart thudding in her ears. All was quiet so she crept closer and pressed her ear carefully to the wooden door. Then his voice sounded and Dani nearly leapt into the air. She only let her breath out when she realised he was on the phone.

Who could he be talking to at one in the morning? A nasty combination of guilt and jealousy clawed at her as she wondered about the special woman in his life. Perhaps it was a long-distance love affair and that's why he was calling so late. *Hi, honey, I kissed someone today…*.

But it was soon apparent this was a business call—exciting business. From what she could make out, he was in the middle of a live auction, bidding by phone. When she heard him murmur "Five million," her decorum abandoned her and she straightened and inched forward, snaking her head around the door.

Quinn sat at his desk, the phone to his ear. She felt the leap of interest as his eyes swivelled toward her, a palpable, inescapable sense of awareness, zeroing in on her. He'd rolled his shirtsleeves up to his elbows and undone his top buttons. One hand rested on a file in front of him, under a half-full glass of some amber liquid. The desk lamp was on, but otherwise the room was in darkness.

Dani lingered in the shadows, although he gave no sign that he was either displeased or happy with her presence. But he did not release her from his gaze. She leaned against the door, her heart thudding along in the silences that punctuated his infrequent responses.

After a couple of minutes, Quinn sipped his drink and then laid the receiver down and turned the speaker phone on, all without taking his eyes off her face. She took that as something of an invitation. Here was an opportunity to have a glimpse into his world, see the negotiator at work.

She moved a few steps farther into the room and rested her hands on the edge of a chair to keep that barrier between them.

The voice on the speaker was unmistakably English. She heard the name of a well-known auction house and the words *lot seven*. Presumably the auction was being conducted in London. Dani wondered if the man on the phone was a bid clerk from the auction house or an employee of Quinn's.

The item being bid for was a famous painting by a contemporary Irish artist who'd died in the sixties. She only knew that because Howard had one of his paintings. She wasn't sure how many bidders there were for this particular item. The bids were relayed to Quinn as they happened, although Dani heard nothing of the activity in the auction house, only the man's voice. The pauses in between bids seemed interminable. They probably weren't, but she guessed there was a lot of tension on the other side of the world. Lord knows there was enough in this office.

Would he smile if he won the bid? Celebrate with a drink? She held his gaze, and no doubt her face was alive with questions. His, however, was framed in intense concentration that held her captive.

The price was now up to eight million pounds. Dani

inched a little closer to the desk, marvelling at his calm. It probably wasn't his money he was spending, but if it'd been her, she would have buckled under the pressure. The next million took only two or three minutes to be disposed of. Still Quinn looked at her face.

"Ten million pounds, sir?"

He didn't flinch, but she did. While she'd been thinking about him, about his face and concentration and possible means of celebration, she had waylaid a couple of million.

Quinn quietly affirmed.

Ten million! That was *how* much in Australian dollars? For a painting?

The next pause was a long one. Dani was halfway across the room now, just a few more steps to the chair in front of his desk.

"The other party has just bid eleven, Mr. Everard."

"You may proceed," Quinn said quietly, and flexed the fingers of his right hand.

Dani covered her mouth with her hand and moved to the desk. The tension was killing her, but how cool he was. No sign of emotion crossed his features. He might have been reading the paper.

The minutes crawled by. Twelve million came and went. Her throat felt like sandpaper and she swallowed. Quinn lifted the glass and moistened his lips, then held it out to her.

Cognac. She would never smell it again without remembering this night. It slid down her throat and washed her lungs with heat. Slowly she rolled the glass over her forehead before setting it down on the desk. She had to lean well forward to get it within his reach, so she edged one hip onto the desk, twisting around to face him.

His eyes were inscrutable. A trickle of sweat began its journey down her spine, surprising her. She arched a little as the fabric of her silky robe slid over and cooled the moisture. A tiny flicker of that mahogany gaze told her he'd noticed, but not one muscle in his face twitched.

"Mr. Everard," the bid clerk's nasal voice intoned. "The other party has entered into a consultation with his client. Are you happy to hold?"

"Yes."

Dani's breath gushed out and she stretched her tense limbs and rubbed the back of her neck, thankful for the intermission.

"By the way, Quinn…" The man on the line lowered and warmed his voice. "That commodity you were interested in? A blank wall so far, I'm afraid. However…"

Quinn shifted but made no response to her raised brows. "Go on."

"A gentleman of my acquaintance has recently returned from visiting the big house on the other side of town. He owes me certain favours."

Quinn chuckled. "You run with the most appalling crowd, Maurice."

"I will let you know directly if I can be of any further assistance," There was a muffled crackle and muted voices. "I think we are ready to resume, sir."

"Thank you," Quinn murmured, his eyes back on Dani's face.

She lost the ability to judge time in the airless room. The performance may have lasted ten minutes or an hour. The last two million pounds advanced and Dani took another sip of liquor, her nipples prickling with the knowledge that he watched her every move. Rather than push the glass across the desk, she walked around to his side, placed it in front of him and leaned against the desk beside him. Quinn swivelled in his chair to face her, still holding her prisoner with his eyes.

Fourteen million pounds.

Dani swallowed.

Fourteen-point-two million. The other bidder had opted to chop the bid. Quinn offered no objection, neither did the auctioneer, apparently. Dani cleared her dry throat and helped herself to another sip of cognac while he watched.

Fourteen-point-five million. The room spun a little, which could have been the cognac. It was like a vacuum in here. Quinn Everard stared at her calmly, steadily, and the bid rose another massive increment. The tension was unbearable.

The skin of her throat and face tickled and she swiped at it, somehow agitated and afraid for him. She could not even contemplate him losing now, not after this. Not when she felt so sensitised, so aware of his gaze gripping her, holding her up.

Fourteen-point-seven million pounds for lot seven, going once. She chewed on her thumbnail, praying. Her chest rose and fell as each breath tortured her lungs.

Fourteen-point-seven million pounds for lot seven, going twice. Dani sucked in a massive breath, held it. This was it!

It was over! Quinn had won the bid.

Air gushed out from her lungs and she slumped momentarily, but then elation poured through her like the most illicit rush. She leapt in the air, her arms high above her head, her hands fisted in victory. For the first time in many minutes, maybe even an hour, Quinn was not looking at her. He stared at the file on the desk. His shoulders were rigid.

"Congratulations, Mr. Everard, and thank you for participating."

He exhaled slowly. "Thank you, Maurice." He paused, as if about to add something, but then looked up into Dani's face. "Thank you," he repeated, and she saw that his teeth were clenched. His hand shot out and hit the switch of the phone. Then he was standing in front of her, gripping her waist hard. He dragged her forward into him, his body like stone against her soft, yielding form.

She wrapped her arms around his neck and sagged against him, burying her face in his shoulder. Quinn moved so that her head tilted up, her throat exposed.

Bite me, she thought, her blood screaming in her ears. She was leaping out of her skin. Never had she reached this peak of excitement in her life, and she couldn't begin to think of consequences, other women, her heart, his hatred for Howard.

As if he'd heard her plea, Quinn lowered his head and nuzzled the hollow at the base of her throat briefly, then took her mouth hard. The taste of leather and almonds from aged cognac filled her mouth. His need for her came from farther down where his groin pushed into the silk-clad vee of her thighs. With a strangled gasp, she pushed back, feeling the distended ridge of his fly, every link of his zipper.

His tongue lashed hers, teeth knocked and scraped. She gasped breathlessly when his hand cupped and squeezed her buttock, forcing her forward. Then his hand ran down the short robe and to the sensitive back of her thigh, lifting it high and hard against him, so that her leg came up and wrapped around his hip. Her mind splintered with a desperate need of carnal contact.

She got it in spades, and the more she jerked against him, the higher she went. Grinding and straining, she became something—someone—she had no control over. She was on a collision course with a cyclone, building higher with every lash of his tongue deep in her mouth and every hard, fast thrust against her hot centre. And then he gripped the soft inside of her leg from behind and moved up, his seeking fingers sending a bolt of fiery energy searing through her. She lost the battle to be aware of her actions or his. All she knew was a wave of scalding pleasure that fisted and ebbed and fisted again and again, driving everything out of her mind.

She sagged against him, trying without success to halt the slide of her leg down his. Boneless, still swimming in pleasure, she trusted him to hold her up because her only tenuous grip was one hand around his neck. The other arm was behind her, palm pressed into the desk and trembling.

Quinn dragged her thong down her legs and made short work of the knot of her robe. While she still lagged, he plunged his hand into her hair and lifted her face to his.

His eyes snapped at her, fierce and hot. "Again."

"Yes." She sucked air into her lungs and pushed up off the desk and the madness started again.

Hands tore at clothing, mouths scraped over heated flesh, breath gushed from screaming lungs. When she got her hands inside his shirt, they slid on his slicked flesh. Cool, calm Quinn Everard was sweating, her mind crowed. She had reduced him to this, a wild animal desperate to copulate, so far removed from the suave, sophisticated businessman he was.

Where had she come from, this wanton, panting woman using her teeth and nails, taking his tongue into her mouth as if it was a drug she was addicted to? She was a nice girl about sex, only did it with someone she really cared about. One didn't do nasty sex when one had lived in a fishbowl all one's life, just like one didn't do drugs or drunken rampages, either.

"Do it!" the nice girl panted, desperate to have all of him now.

His hands tangled in her hair. "You think I have any control over this?" he gasped, holding her face up and scowling down into her eyes. "That went when you walked into the room."

The only answer she was capable of giving was to pull his torso against her and swipe her breasts back and forth, again and again. His crisp chest hair scraped and burned her nipples, spurring her into intensifying her efforts with his pants fastening. She finally got his pants down and at last he was naked, in all his pure, proud, masculine glory, roped with muscle, rough with hair, fierce with need.

There was a brief halt when he clapped a hand to his head. "Wallet?" Feverishly, he picked up his pants, slapping the pockets, then his face cleared and he reached behind her to the drawer and drew his wallet out.

Grateful for his foresight—protection hadn't even occurred to her—she took the pack from him and made it memorable, smoothing the condom over his hot, hard flesh with a dedication that had both of them holding their breaths for long seconds. He was built. Even her wildest daydreams hadn't done him justice. Then he groaned and grabbed her hands in a viselike grip. This agitated man before her, streaked with sweat and with rumpled hair, was a side of him she could come to like. But right now, her body was screaming for him, she needed more than *like*.

Then his palms were covering her breasts and his mouth was stealing her breath and the eye of the storm moved on, throwing them into a sexual frenzy again.

Quinn kept one arm firmly around her back for support while the other swept clear the surface of his desk. Then down she went, clutching at his shoulders and arms, dragging him down, too. Limbs tangled, teeth gnashed, her heart threatened to explode out of her chest. The storm overtook her, both of them. The air was filled with grunts and bumps and harshly drawn breaths. He dug his fingers into her hips and dragged her forward. She felt heat meeting heat and then the delicious, brimming slide of his total invasion. For a second, the absolute shock and pleasure of him deep inside immobilised her. Then she strained up, locked her legs around him and held on for the ride of her life. He kept one arm under her to shield her from the unforgiving desk. The other he plunged into her hair, pulling her head back to give him access to her mouth. Bodies and mouths locked together, she threw herself heart and soul into a coupling so intense, as full of the fire and brilliance of the diamond upstairs, that she wondered if they'd survive or just combust.

Her second orgasm slammed into her, making her falter and lose her rhythm. Her legs relaxed suddenly from around him, splaying wide as coils of sensation pumped and flowed to every extremity. She sobbed with delight and Quinn straightened a little, lifted her higher, changing the angle to drive new pleasure into her. She was assailed by so much sensation, she couldn't contain it and was swept away in another inferno of red-hot pleasure that never cooled, only soared higher. Somehow she held on, lifting her legs around his waist again, rising to meet him, until she felt the change in his grip intensify, his arms becoming so rigid, her hands lost purchase. But he gathered her whole body to him, right off the desk, threw his head back and in a groaning rush of breath that went on and on, he pumped, again and again, and then collapsed on top of her.

Minutes later sometime in the next millennium, Dani stirred and tried lifting her head. She was trapped with Quinn's face buried in her hair on one side. It was an interesting predicament, unable to move, the harsh light of the desk lamp only inches away, burning her face and revealing all her flaws, no doubt. Quinn's heartbeat, right on top of hers, rattled away at an impossible rate. She swivelled her eyes to the side, saw the devastation on the floor, clothes mixed with papers and with cognac.

Her hair scratched and whispered on the white blotter pad. She blew softly into his ear, repeating the gesture when there was no response. His lashes flickered and he turned his head and licked his lips. Slowly his eyes focussed on her.

"You okay?" he asked weakly.

Dani's dry lips stretched in a strained smile. Oh, man, was she ever!

He blinked apologetically, lifting his torso a couple of inches. "Sorry. I'm squashing you."

Quinn Everard was embarrassed, she thought. Like her, he probably didn't do nasty sex.

That made her smile wider. "I never took you for a desk man."

He blinked, looking appalled. "I'm not. I'm…sorry. Did I hurt you?"

She bit back a full-on smile. "Only if you call pleasure pain."

They shifted jerkily, which brought about an interesting sensation since he was still inside her. He lifted a little higher and ran his eyes down her body, making her squirm. Distracted by her belly button jewellery, he tugged lightly on the barbell she wore; a triangular knot of sterling silver, studded with deep red Swarovski Austrian crystals. "Did you make this? It's very pretty."

Dani made belly button jewellery only for herself. The precious stones she preferred working with were too expensive, since they were destined, for the most part, to be hidden under clothing.

His big hand, spread wide, covered her belly, then moved slowly up to pass lightly over the tips of her breasts. She squeezed around him, as tight as she could, pleasuring them both. Smiling, he bent his head and tongued a rapidly hardening nipple, even as she felt him harden inside her.

"I think I can dredge up some finesse, if you'd consider giving me a second chance."

"While I have nothing at all against the desk man—" she smiled and put her arms around his neck, arching up into him "—I wouldn't be averse to some finesse in the very near future."

Six

Quinn declared the next day a holiday to celebrate the results of the auction. He'd made all the arrangements by the time she'd showered, and within the hour, they were at Port Douglas Marina boarding a bareboat charter catamaran named *Seawind,* a ten-metre flared-hull beauty with mainsail.

They sailed out to the Low Isles and snorkelled around the breathtaking underwater garden of the Great Barrier Reef. But by late morning, the area was overrun by hordes of tourists on day trips, so they set sail for a small inlet to put into and enjoy the hamper the charter company provided.

The weather was perfect, calm and clear. Quinn was happy to find that on the water the humidity didn't bother him at all. Either that or he was becoming acclimatised.

"This is the life." Dani appeared from below deck with her lime-green sundress on again; he liked the bikini better but she'd burn easily with her skin. And at least he now knew exactly what was under that dress. It would give him something to do later, peeling it off her....

He offered her a plate and glass from the hamper and she stretched her legs out along the seat, sighing with pleasure.

"Ever sailed before?" he asked.

"No. Howard was never interested in boats."

Quinn popped a cheese-topped cracker in his mouth. "Did you get on?"

"With Howard?" She considered. "Most of the time. He wasn't averse to sharing his opinion on clothes, friends, music and so on, but I suppose that was his right since he paid the bills."

She unscrewed the cap of the chilled sauvignon blanc wine and held it up to him.

Quinn had his mouth full but shook his head, holding up a bottle of water instead.

Dani leaned back on the seat with her wine and a plate of nibbles. "He was kinder to me than to the others. I was never going to run his company, so I guess he went easier on me."

"He bought the shop for you, didn't he?"

"It was a loan, one I've nearly paid off."

"Why do you think they never married?" Quinn really wanted to know why the bastard never publicly acknowledged Dani as his daughter.

"Who?" She looked blank.

"Your mother and Howard."

She took a sip of wine, her brow wrinkling. "Why would they marry? He was her brother-in-law."

"They obviously liked each other well enough to stay together all those years," he mused aloud.

"They were a bit like an old married couple, I suppose, when he wasn't out putting it around..." She grinned.

"But she still stayed?" Don't tell him Sonya wasn't in for all she could get. Quinn had never met Sonya Hammond, but the Sydney press had long speculated on the relationship between the womanising Howard Blackstone and his sister-in-law. No matter how often the Blackstone publicity machine denied it, Dani's paternity was subject to debate on a regular basis. Most— Quinn included—assumed she was Howard's love child.

"I know everyone thought Mum was his mistress," Dani said moodily. "I've lived with the scandalised looks and whispers all my life. But my mum has more class in her little finger than all of them."

"But there was you." If Howard didn't want to acknowledge his love child, why did he flaunt them, keep them in his house?

Her gaze was unwavering, if a little cool. "Howard's not my father," she said tiredly. "Look, I know you hate him and I know he has—had—his faults. But he looked after us." She looked down, picking at the hem of her dress. "Which is a lot more than can be said for my real father."

"Who is...?"

"Who cares?" she shot back. "Not him, that's for sure."

Quinn held up his hands, remembering the cliché about redheads and temper. "Sorry. Touchy subject, huh?"

He sympathised but was still reeling a little to find she wasn't Blackstone's daughter. That was a turn up for the books.

"Not touchy, boring." Her voice dropped. "He didn't want us. End of story." She stared moodily out at nothing but sea, and the sun glinted off her copper curls. "I wouldn't have minded very much if Howard was my father. At least he was there."

Quinn supposed he should feel guilty. Sleeping with Dani wasn't a victory over the old man, after all. Regardless, it still felt damn good.

And then she smiled brilliantly, unfolded those glorious legs and came to stand close and rummage through the hamper. "Who taught you to sail?"

"My father." Quinn spent many a Saturday morning on the water as a kid until his parents decided the boat was a luxury and the money would be better spent elsewhere.

"Was it very rough, growing up in a foster home?"

"Rough?" He smiled. "Sometimes. Bloody noisy. It was more or less open house. I doubt even Mum and Dad knew how many kids were under the roof at any one time."

"You called them Mum and Dad?"

"They are my mum and dad," Quinn said, bemused.

"Well, yes, but how long were you with them?" She looked confused.

Quinn scratched his head. "All my life. I think you've got the wrong end of the stick. I wasn't a foster kid. All the other kids were."

Dani's face cleared. "Oh, I see. So you and your parents ran a foster home?"

"Something like that," Quinn agreed. "They have a big old villa in Newtown, off King Street. Lots of rooms, all in various states of disrepair, and a kitchen that's the size of a hotel dining room."

"Not at all what I imagined for you."

She moved back to her seat, but her enticing floral scent lingered and he sniffed carefully, keeping it for himself. "What did you imagine?"

Dani grinned. "A grand old mansion with a butler. Everybody dressed for dinner and speaking very *na-i-cely*." She gave an apologetic shrug. "Sorry but you're just so damned refined."

Quinn chuckled. "My parents would love that. They are the most unpretentious people I know. Old hippies, very socially aware. They don't care about money or nice things, only sharing what they have with the less fortunate." He paused. "I'm sure I embarrass them, successful capitalist that I am. Not that they don't hit me up every couple of months with some harebrained fundraising scheme or other."

She crossed one shapely leg over the other, snagging his attention, holding it for seconds. What was this hold she had over him? She was younger than him by seven years, but that wasn't the allure. He'd found her his equal in maturity and intelligence.

"You must have seen some sad things, though."

"Kids are selfish." He opened his bottle of water. "I was too busy marking my territory."

"Is that how you broke your nose?"

Quinn gave her a resigned smile. "Yep. That was Jake Vance, actually."

"Jake?" She sat up.

"You know him?" Something in him bristled. He'd be surprised if she didn't know of Jake; he was one of the most talked-about entrepreneurs in Australia. But as he was his best friend and also quite the ladies' man, Quinn wasn't sure if he liked the idea of Jake and Dani being friendly.

"Not very well. I met him a couple of times. He was at Kim and Ric's wedding, with Briana Davenport, actually, pre-Jarrod."

Quinn nodded, relaxing. "I'd heard that."

"Tell me about the broken nose," Dani prompted.

"We didn't see eye to eye when he first came to stay." Quinn absently rubbed the bridge of his nose, recalling the mother of all his teenage fights.

"Jake Vance was a foster child?" She sounded disbelieving.

He supposed it was difficult to think of Jake like that when the whole country associated him with immense wealth.

"Not exactly. He had a mother, but there were some problems, mostly to do with his stepfather. He ran away from home, looking for work in the city and things didn't pan out the way he'd hoped. Ma and Pa got to talking to him on the streets one day so he turned up at home."

Quinn as a teenager was well used to sharing but liked to be asked nicely. Jake didn't ask nicely. Quinn wasn't about to lose his standing as top dog in his own house. The battle was epic, and at the end of it, neither boy could stand. And that was the start of a long and valued friendship.

"He's my closest friend now. He and Lucy my foster sister. She was abused from the start. Came to us when she was eight and just stayed." He caught her horrified look. "She and Jake had a thing a few years back, but now she lives in London. Corporate banker," he finished proudly.

"How awful." Dani shuddered. "What makes people such monsters?"

"I don't suppose people start out that way," Quinn said thoughtfully. "But it's not that hard to be careful if you don't want a baby."

Dani nodded sadly, and he realised that was probably close to the bone for her. "Not these days, anyway," he qualified, not meaning to suggest her mother and the mystery lover had been careless.

"So have the things you've seen and heard put you off having kids?" Her voice trailed off when a shadow passed over his face. "Oh, I'm sorry, Quinn." Dani looked very uncomfortable suddenly.

"That's okay. I was married, yes."

"I remembered as soon as I'd asked. Laura Hartley, wasn't it? I only know because she was at PLC around the same time as Kim. I was a couple of years after."

"Ah." He nodded. "I didn't know that." PLC— Pymble Ladies College, a private college on the North Shore—had an excellent academic reputation, but it was strictly for rich kids.

"I'm sorry," Dani repeated quietly. "I remember now hearing that she'd died."

Quinn stared out over the waves. "We married when we were still at university. Laura wanted to be a social worker, whereas her parents…" his voice hardened as he continued, "They had other ideas. Sure, they sent her to a nice school and tolerated her going to uni, but they didn't intend their daughter to get her hands dirty. She was only marking time till the right rich husband came along." He smiled bitterly. "When she moved in with me on the cheap side of town, her family disowned her."

"What was the family business again?" Dani's brow wrinkled. "I remember they had stores all over the country. I think they were friends with Howard."

"Soft furnishings." Quinn swallowed, but it didn't erase the familiar burn of anger that flared up at the mention of Howard's name. He may not have caused Laura's death, but he sure influenced how she felt in those last days.

"How old was she when she died?"

"Twenty-six. It was sudden, only a few months from the first symptoms till the end."

"I'm so sorry," she said again, her golden eyes pools of sympathy.

"Don't be. I wouldn't swap those few years for anything, not a bit of it." He leaned forward and poured a little wine into a glass, mindful that he was skippering the boat. "She loved our life, my parents. She loved that we took in the unwanted and the street kids." Some of the good times flooded in, making him smile. "Every time I turned around, she was sitting in a corner, talking to some snot-nosed kid. They confided in her, told her everything.

More than Mum and Dad, even." He looked down at the wine in his glass, swirled it around before tossing it down in one gulp. "That was the hell of it. She would have gone places, helped so many. Why she had to die is beyond me."

It was his one taste of true failure. He couldn't understand how it could happen, how she could be taken.

How could he not have saved her?

He rubbed his chin. Part of him would always love Laura, or more accurately, love that time of his life, when he was young and silly enough to believe in forever, believe he and Laura were invincible.

But Howard Blackstone had tainted the memories. He'd never forgive him for that.

And as he tried and failed to swallow the hard knot of bitterness, he found himself wanting to justify it to Dani. He called himself a swine for doing it, for doing what Howard had done to him. Tainting the memories.

But he wanted her to know. "You want to know why I hate Howard so much?"

Dani blinked at his harsh tone.

"The bastard ruined the last weeks of Laura's life."

She visibly paled. "I didn't know he knew her."

"He didn't. But you're right about him being friends with the Hartleys. After the World Association of Diamonds vote went against him, he did all he could to blacken my name. That was fine, I could take care of myself. Laura always had faith her folks would come around and accept our marriage. But with Blackstone whispering in their ears, filling them full of hate, they turned their backs, even knowing she was terminal."

Dani's mouth dropped open in dismay, and she looked away as if she couldn't bear to look at his face. Yes, it hurts, doesn't it, he thought bitterly. She'd thought Howard was some kind of saint. Well, now she knew differently.

"When everything went to hell and the tumour came back, I went to them, begged them to come. Not that we ever gave up hope..." Laura would not permit anyone to think for a minute she wouldn't beat the cancer. "But they tossed me out. They said Howard had told them all about me. How I couldn't be trusted, how I was after her money, how she was my meal ticket out of the slums." His head rolled back and he breathed deeply of the warm air. "They couldn't even give her peace at the end," he said with disgust.

"I—I didn't know."

How could she?

Now that the anger was out, as always, it quickly faded. Time did that. Blackstone had a black heart and that wasn't Dani's fault. It seemed even being six feet under was no barrier to hurting people.

"They didn't deserve her, Quinn," she said quietly. "You did."

He sighed, thinking that Dani had her own problems. At least he had great family support. He suspected she'd never felt part of a real family. He'd glimpsed a vulnerability in her, an insecurity. He remembered it from long ago, when he used to notice such things. Loneliness, a need to belong.

Somewhere along the way, he'd just plain stopped looking.

The hell with it. Today was a rare day, one that didn't come along very often. She was sexy, fun, talented. Available. Why was he wallowing in the bitter past? And in some ways, telling Dani was kind of cathartic. She knew the man, knew his faults. She gave him a slightly different perspective.

Quinn would never forgive or forget, but he could let go a little more. That's what time did. And the fact that she wasn't Howard's daughter had to be a good thing, right?

He set his glass down, sorry that he'd made her sad. He wanted the warmth of her brilliant smile back, and perhaps he wanted to warm her a little also. When he held out his hand to her, she smiled up at him and he saw understanding and empathy. When he bent to kiss the soft, fragrant flesh just under her earlobe, her skin steamed up quickly and her pulse quickened under his mouth.

This was about sex, he reminded himself. Unbelievable and uncomplicated sex. If it made them feel good and if no one expected anything more, where was the harm?

He lifted his head to see her mouth turned up in sultry understanding. Quinn resolved to give her as good as she gave.

He pulled her to her feet and downstairs to the cabin, peeling her clothing off on the way. The salt from her skin tingled on his tongue as he revealed and then tasted every delicious inch of her. He made her stand still, legs braced, and made love to her with his mouth. She rocked on her heels with the sway of the vessel under them, clutching his head. His bitterness and her insecurities melted away as he tipped her onto the bed, slid deep into her body and looked into her eyes, and they became one with the motion of the sea.

"How's it going?"

Dani looked up from her workbench, where, days later, she was once again engrossed. "Today I start on the chain."

She was working with platinum, always a challenge but one she enjoyed. Many jewellers found the metal too soft and dense to work with, but with practice, it got easier and the rewards were worth it.

"You chose diamond cut and not snake," he noted approvingly.

Dani nodded. "It's classic and doesn't kink so much." She picked up her torch again and resumed her work. Quinn pulled up a stool. It was becoming a habit of his to come in here and watch her work. He seemed fascinated by the whole process.

"It must be exciting to create something from start to finish and know it will outlive you." He was flicking through her portfolio again, he did that a lot. On every page, he found something that interested him and would ask her how she decided on that particular combination of texture or colour. She broke all the rules, he told her, and yet her jewellery worked beautifully.

Dani was buoyed by his interest. He really seemed to get her, to share her vision of the relationship between gemstones and precious metals. Being a designer was a solitary occupation. Most people were only interested in the end product, not the journey of creation. It was nice to have someone to share ideas with for once.

Several days had passed since the boat trip, each one slightly cooler and calmer as the fitful cyclone season waned and autumn woke up. Dani barely noticed the weather since she only left the workroom to finalise a few last-minute wedding arrangements for Ryan and Jessica or to make love with Quinn.

She glanced over to where he sat at the desk, flicking through her portfolio. So far she'd shied away from badgering him on the intended recipient of the yellow diamond. He was an honourable man, despite the coercion he'd used at the start. She had to believe that. A loyal man who wouldn't make promises and trifle with her feelings.

It wasn't her normal way of doing things, but she had to be grown-up about it. One disastrous relationship had only added to her lifelong feeling of not being good enough, firmly entrenched in second best. But that wasn't Quinn's problem. They were from different worlds. This wasn't a "relationship" so much as a "situation"—and as far as situations went, it wasn't a bad one to be in.

So long as she didn't try to make it into something else.

Her phone rang and she put her torch down. It was Steve from the shop to say Matt Hammond was there to see her. She gave him the beach house address and prepared to meet her cousin for the first time, face-to-face. Several minutes later, understandably nervous, she let Quinn answer the door while she hovered a few steps back.

"Danielle?" Matt Hammond looked from one to the other, a confused look on his handsome face. "I didn't realise you knew each other," he said, taking Quinn's proffered hand.

Quinn stepped back and motioned her forward with a reassuring smile. "Dani's doing a little designing job for me."

She looked up into Matt's face. He was nearly as tall as Quinn, leaner, with thick sandy hair and sharp grey eyes that reminded her of her mother's.

"Come in and sit down." Quinn led the way to the living area, offered refreshments and then discreetly withdrew.

Dani twisted her hands together, unsure of the reason for his visit, hoping it was a genuine overture to get to know the Australian side of his family. Her first tentative questions concerned Blake. It was a tricky subject after the months of speculation about his late wife's infidelity and his son's paternity. But when she asked if he had a photo, like any proud father, he produced several from his wallet.

The snapshots showed a dark, rather serious-looking little boy. "Three and a half," Matt responded to Dani's query about his age. She dredged up the courage to ask if she could have one to send to her mother and Matt readily handed over a couple.

"Are you here on holiday?"

"I thought it was time we met," he said simply. "I also wanted to talk to Quinn, but had no idea I'd find you together."

Dani felt her cheeks glow. "As he said," she quickly inserted, "I'm helping him with a designing project."

"Good for you." Matt smiled. "A recommendation

from Quinn Everard is a valuable thing in this business. I saw the catalogue for the February launch, by the way. Your pieces were impressive."

Dani beamed. She'd had a lot of work as a direct result of the Blackstone launch, proving that Howard, who'd talked her into being the featured designer, had known his stuff.

But best not to mention that name in this company, she thought.

"And that is another reason I'm here," Matt continued. "You've heard, I suppose, that four of the Heart of the Outback diamonds have been returned to me?"

Dani nodded cautiously, noting his use of the Heart of the Outback—the Hammond diamond—as opposed to the Blackstone Rose diamonds.

"I have an idea and I'd like you to be part of it."

Her response was measured. Was this a ploy to upset the Blackstones? "In what way?"

"I want to make an heirloom necklace from the Heart of the Outback diamonds, to be kept in the Hammond family and worn by future Hammond brides."

Dani's mouth dropped open. "Matt, that's a wonderful idea!"

"Hopefully my father will think so, too."

She nodded. Bringing the Heart of the Outback stones—Jeb's legacy—together again for the next generation of Hammonds would surely ease the old man's bitterness in his last years. "Matt, my mother would so love to restore some sort of relationship with Oliver and your mother, and you and Blake, too. Do you think there is any hope of that?"

Matt's silvery gaze was steady and open. "I have no problem with Sonya, Danielle. But there is a lot of water under that bridge and I can't speak for Dad." Then his voice softened. "Small steps? Starting with you designing the Bridal Rose necklace?"

The Bridal Rose. Emotion almost overwhelmed her. "It would be an honour," she mumbled, staring fixedly at Blake's photos to hide a sheen of tears.

Although she was close to her cousins Kim and Ryan, and had never doubted her mother's love, finding a place she felt she belonged had always eluded her. To have found a new family and have a part in reuniting its members was a privilege. She and Matt seemed to click, just as she and Jarrod had.

Then a more selfish elation sneaked up on her. First, the beautiful yellow diamond upstairs in the safe, and now the pink Blackstone Rose diamonds. What were the chances of being offered two commissions with stones of this calibre? And at only twenty-seven years old! "What a pity the fifth diamond hasn't come to light."

"I'm working on that," Matt said mysteriously. "In the meantime, I'd like you to design the necklace as if there *were* a fifth diamond—the centrepiece. Can you do that?"

"Of course. Can you give me a couple more weeks to finish what I'm doing here?"

He acquiesced. "I hadn't thought further ahead than getting an answer from you."

"Well, you have it." She smiled happily. "I would love to do it. And I'm rapt you thought of me."

Matt's smile was slow to start but it lit up his face.

"You are a very talented designer and a Hammond. The perfect choice."

They talked for an hour about the jewellery trade and little Blake, and ended on his brother Jarrod's recent engagement to Briana. Dani thought it must be strange for Matt to see his brother marry his late wife's sister, but Matt confided he'd always been fond of Briana. More relaxed now, she mentioned the rumours doing the rounds a few weeks ago, suggesting Jarrod Hammond was really the missing Blackstone heir. To her relief, Matt did not seem offended at hearing the Blackstone name.

"Jarrod's birth mother may have something to say about that," he retorted.

Dani was surprised. There had been no mention of Jarrod's birth mother in the newspaper stories.

Matt's mouth tightened. "I've met her. She taps Jarrod up for money every so often, then disappears under whatever rock she crawled out from."

Her heart went out to Jarrod. Impossibly handsome, a successful lawyer, a beautiful new fiancée, and yet that suave exterior hid its own personal pain.

But at least he knew who his mother was….

As if her cousin had recognised her momentary sadness, he turned it on its head by agreeing to talk to his brother about a family get-together soon. "Briana has dragged him along on one of her modelling assignments overseas. Poor beggar." He pulled an amused face. "But maybe when they get back, we can have a bit of a get-together."

It was tentative but, still, it was an overture. "And Blake?" she asked. "And my mother, too?"

"Why not?"

The three of them had a wonderful dinner at a famous outdoor restaurant in the middle of a copse of huge tropical palms. Quinn toasted her when he heard about the Bridal Rose commission, saying it would really put her on the map in the designing world.

He turned to Matt. "I thought I had a lead on the fifth diamond, but the trail has gone cold, I'm afraid. I'll keep you posted."

Matt was clearly disappointed but still raised his glass to both of them. "I appreciate it, Quinn. Someone must know something. And Danielle, I am looking forward to working with you on the necklace, hopefully with all five stones."

It was truly one of the best days she'd ever had. Her mother would be over the moon that Matt had made contact, and to have the opportunity to rewrite the history of the Heart of the Outback Diamond was such a buzz. To think Quinn might have a hand in locating the fifth stone… It was the perfect end to the perfect day.

Until she walked in on them talking business some time later on her way back from the bathroom. She wasn't eavesdropping, but one palm tree looked much like another and she came in from a different direction to find Matt had moved into her seat and they had their heads together. Something made her pause behind the nearest trunk when she heard the name Blackstone.

"I have already spoken to three of the minor shareholders," Matt said. "If you were to get behind us…"

She heard Quinn's voice. "If you're serious about

this, you need Jake Vance on board, not me. I only have a handful of shares."

"I'm meeting with Jake next week, but listen, they're on shaky ground. The Blackstone empire is crumbling with Howard gone. Perrini and Ryan snap and snarl at each other and Kim spends all her time calming them down. I just want to keep the pressure on."

Dani's rosy wine-glow faded fast, leaving a nasty feeling that her cousin wasn't playing fair.

She waited to hear how her lover responded.

"I'm not interested in a dogfight, Matt. My few shares are performing adequately."

Dani relaxed a little and peeked around the tree trunk.

Matt had leaned back and put his hands behind his head. "I thought you'd jump at the chance to shaft a Blackstone, given your history."

Quinn frowned. "My beef was with Howard, not Blackstone Diamonds."

"Or," Matt continued nonchalantly, "maybe you're mixing business with pleasure."

She saw Quinn's eyes glint dangerously and couldn't expel her next breath.

His voice was low and cool and she had to strain to hear him. "Dani is private business, all right?"

Though her heart was beating loud and fast, mostly for fear of discovery, she heard Matt apologise. "But if I can get Vance on side, you'll go with us?"

"If Jake says sell, I'll sell."

She stayed behind the tree for a few more seconds, trying to make sense of all the emotions. She felt strangely buoyant that Quinn hadn't denied there was something between them. Keenly disappointed that Matt Hammond clearly wasn't ready to embrace the reconciliation of the two family factions just yet. Would he ever be?

And somehow uneasy that she was consorting with the enemy. Perhaps two of them.

Seven

"Quinn, have you heard a rumour about a corporate takeover of Blackstone Diamonds?"

His eyes snapped open. That was out of left field.

Quinn had been lying in bed, idly thinking that his sporadic sexual encounters rarely involved morning sex, especially dreamy morning sex with the same woman. He was always rushing off to a meeting or a flight. Maybe he'd been missing out all these years.

Now he abandoned his reverie to answer Dani. "You stopped screaming your delight one minute ago and suddenly you want to talk business?"

She lay with her head on his chest, her hair a riot of curls against his skin.

Quinn turned his head to look at the clock. Seven-thirty. Time he was up. "Yes, I have heard something. You want coffee or are you staying in bed?"

But she was persistent. "Do you think Matt is involved?"

Had she heard something last night?

Matt's request to sell his shares or support a takeover bid had not surprised him; Quinn had heard he was polling all the Blackstone shareholders for support. He was getting it, too.

But not from him, at least not yet. His fingers rasped over his chin. "What is this inquisition before I've had my coffee?"

She kept her face down on his chest, a fact he found strangely worrying.

"I heard you," she said in a small voice. "Last night at the restaurant. Talking about selling your shares in Blackstone."

Quinn's eyes narrowed in the dim room. Scratch all those nice thoughts about waking up with the same woman. He didn't know whether to laugh or be offended. Who the hell did she think she was? "Eavesdropping, Danielle? If you heard us, you'd know I turned him down."

She lifted her head and looked him right in the face. And it hit him: she was serious.

The urge to laugh disappeared. "A company takeover," he said, twisting his finger around a springy red curl, "is very complicated. It needs the support of the board and the requisite number of shares. I'm Little League in Blackstones, Dani."

That was the truth. He had very few shares himself. But he knew Matt was in for more than the Blackstones knew about—and climbing. And Quinn knew who else had a substantial portfolio.

"But if Jake Vance asks you to sell…?"

Quinn stilled. She had heard everything. And she was right out of line. He was not in the habit of justifying himself to anyone, let alone a woman he'd known for a week or so, even if the sex was amazing.

He injected plenty of cool in his reply. "Yes, if he gave me a good enough reason, then I'd sell."

Disappointment darkened her eyes, and just the fact that he recognised that pissed him off. There was no room for emotion in business. That was the dictum that Jake Vance, corporate raider, believed in, and Quinn agreed wholeheartedly, damn it!

"Quinn, what hurts the Blackstones hurts me, you *do* get that, don't you?"

Time to remind both of them this was just a fling. "Just because we're sleeping together, Danielle," he said coldly, "doesn't give you the right to ask about my business dealings."

She flinched. He knew that because he felt it in his chest and stomach, which lay under her torso, in between his legs where she'd squeezed her thigh, over his shoulder where she'd draped one of her arms.

But he held her gaze. He wouldn't negotiate on overstepping boundaries. After a long moment, he nudged her, indicating he wanted to get up. She moved over to her side of the bed. When the hell did they get into his-and-her sides of the bed anyway?

His refection stared balefully back in the bathroom mirror while he wondered what had suddenly happened, what had changed. One minute, he was savouring the delights of a very sexy body. The next, he was wallowing in guilt, thinking about someone else, considering someone else's feelings. Just how deep was he getting here?

Somewhere out on that boat, she'd stirred up some long-buried need to protect. His parents, his childhood home had always been a port in a storm, a harbour for lost and needy souls. Quinn had forgotten what it felt like, until now. Was that what Danielle saw in him? Was she searching for such a port?

He ran the tap and splashed his face, making sure it was good and cold.

This was supposed to be a brief fling, a bit of fun to while away the heat of the day while he was stuck up here in the middle of nowhere. Wanting her every minute of the day in the limited time they had together was acceptable. Thinking about waking up to her every morning was probably teetering on the edge and would have to be addressed—and soon. It had been years since he'd considered relationships and he was perfectly happy with his life just as it was.

But justifying himself to her was definitely off limits.

Steve called at breakfast to ask if Dani could mind the shop for a few hours; he and his partner had an ultrasound to attend. Quinn went into town with her. She was quiet but not snippy, and he had some ideas for marketing he'd been thinking about. He pushed aside the feeling that giving her some decent advice may assuage his guilt somewhat.

"What are you doing here, Dani?" he asked, after a customer walked out with a very nice pair of pearl earrings that she'd gotten for a bargain, he noticed.

Dani looked up from locking the cabinet. "Making a living. Just."

Quinn paced out the tiny interior. The display was funky without being crafty; the quality of her jewellery was too high for that. But the premises were second-rate, security was inadequate and the whole place needed a complete overhaul. "Is it success or failure you're afraid of?"

Dani ran her eye slowly around the shop. "It could use some attention, I know."

"How did you end up here, anyway? Why Port?"

She scratched her neck and shrugged. "It's where I stopped." She picked up a cloth and bottle of glass cleaner and walked out from behind the counter. Today she was almost conservative in below-the-knee tights, high-heeled sandals, a mushroom-coloured tunic with voluminous sleeves and a huge orange silk rose pinned to her lapel.

Why he always noticed her attire was beyond him. He questioned her again. "What were you running from?"

Dani walked to the display cabinet on the other side of the shop and turned her back on him. He heard the hiss of the spray cleaner, saw the sleeves of her creamy shirt rippling as she rubbed and polished. "I was engaged."

As soon as she said it, he remembered a couple of sketchy details. Actually, what he remembered was watching it on a TV news programme and wondering how it qualified as news.

"I was engaged to someone who was convinced, even though I denied it repeatedly, that I was Howard's daughter and, therefore, a Blackstone heiress."

She moved around the cabinet, rubbing intently, but didn't look at him.

"I remember," Quinn murmured, noticing two distinct spots of colour on her cheeks.

"You remember the scandal."

She did look at him then and he saw that it wasn't so much pain setting her mouth into a thin line and colouring her cheeks. It was embarrassment.

"The media had a field day." She gave a tight laugh. "There were some really funny headlines. I would have laughed myself if…" Her eyes slid away and she moved to another glass-topped cabinet. "Do you know, he even demanded his ring back, until Ryan paid him a visit on Howard's orders."

Quinn exhaled. "I'd say you had a lucky escape."

She rolled her eyes and the smile she had forced disappeared. "I just got tired of it. I'm either the illegitimate love child, the scheming gold digger or the poor stupid fool whose fiancé got caught with his pants down. Just one more brush to tar me with."

She fell silent and continued to rub vigorously at some imaginary mark.

"Why here?"

She raised her shoulders. "I love the beach and the climate. It's far enough from Sydney that most people don't even know I'm related to the Blackstones." She glanced at him briefly and grinned. "And I'll admit to a bit of poetic license. The population is pretty transient here. I can be whoever and whatever I want."

Images of a wan face, tamed hair and indeterminate clothing flitted through his mind. He'd seen her featured several times in newspaper spreads or television reports. But he'd never noticed her beauty, her animated smile and sparkle, until he'd met her up here. Now he found himself consciously holding his breath when he heard her come downstairs in the mornings, wondering what jaw-dropping mishmash of colours and textures she would amaze him with today.

Quinn put his hand out. "Come here."

He led her outside and then turned her and gestured to the faded lettering above the door. "What does that say?"

"Dani Hammond. Fine Jeweller of Port Douglas."

"Fine Jeweller," he repeated. "We both know how much study and work experience it takes to be able to put those two words after your name."

He put his hands on her shoulders and turned her to face him. "Is this what you envisaged while you were putting in the work?"

Her head dropped a little. "Not really."

"What did you see?"

"What does anyone see just starting out? I wanted to be the best."

"Didn't you want important people to come to you, celebrities and royalty and private collectors?" he asked.

She pursed her lips. "I suppose…"

"Would Howard Blackstone have put his money up if he thought this was as far as you'd go?"

"Ouch!" Her eyes flashed and Quinn wondered if there might be a little residual anger from this morning.

"This," he said as he turned his palm up to indicate the shop front, "isn't good enough. Not the shop or the location."

He showed her back inside. "You have the connections, Dani. If the Blackstones won't help, invest in a marketing company. Maybe my people can point you in the right direction."

Dani frowned, not convinced. "Listen, I have so many orders from the February launch, I can barely keep up."

But Quinn was pacing again. "You need to move. Sydney..." He caught the negative set of her mouth. "Melbourne, then. Hell, why limit yourself? You're good, Dani, great, even. Why not New York or Europe?"

She put up a hand. "I was thinking of a couple of doors down, actually."

Quinn stopped and looked at her, put off his stride.

"The vacant shop two doors down," she repeated patiently. "It's nearly on the corner of the mall, so there's lots of foot traffic. It's twice the size and very modern."

His head went back and he stared down his nose at her. *Why* wasn't she getting this? "You want to be the best? The best in Port Douglas?"

"Yes, I do remember the one-horse-town comment," she said testily, her cheeks firing up.

"Hey, it's your career. But no one will ever know you if you don't give your profile a kick up the backside."

She stepped up to him, head thrown back, fingers curled into her palms, those golden eyes positively steaming. And Quinn realised, too late, that yes, she really was still sore about this morning.

"I can't be too bad," she said hotly, "since you practically *begged* me to design the necklace for you."

"Hey, it wasn't my idea," he retaliated. "In fact, I argued against you being allowed within ten feet of that diamond."

* * *

It was like a blow to her gut.

This morning he'd inflicted a neat cut, chosen his words carefully to put her in her place. She wasn't to question him, wasn't to expect anything from him.

This was punchier, without preamble or foresight. She realised from the stunned look on his face that he hadn't intended to tell her.

A deathly hush descended. So Quinn Everard wasn't here on the pretext that she was the best designer around. Crushed, she felt the blood drain from her face.

What did she expect? He had only just finished belabouring the point. The best—hah! Who was she kidding? He'd been right, again and again. This wasn't what she'd imagined for herself. Her shop was pathetic, and Howard had given her the loan but never stopped harping on her about moving back to Sydney and getting serious about her career.

Quinn inhaled and opened his mouth to speak, but she had to get in first, before she crumpled. "Who is your client?" she asked quickly.

"Dani, for what it's worth, I now have complete confidence in you."

Fine jeweller, indeed. Somehow she managed to keep her chin steady. "Am I not to know who hired me?"

He shook his head. "I'm sorry."

She should have learned by now never to get ideas above her station. She was second best. Always had been. The stigma of illegitimacy. Nick. Hell, even

Quinn Everard with his designer awards and chain-store quips.

She now felt justified to ask about the woman she was supposedly making the necklace for, a subject she had conveniently put to one side once he started blowing her mind in bed. "The diamond isn't for your girl-friend?"

Quinn looked away. "That was your assumption, one I chose not to correct."

She'd been feeling guilty for an imaginary girl-friend—not that the thought of wrecking someone's life had stopped her, or him. She was just some floozy to while away the hours with up here in the middle of nowhere. He was bored, he was hot. She was available.

Her mother always told her it was okay to make a mistake as long as you learned from it. Obviously Nick's betrayal was no deterrent for making huge lapses of judgement where men were concerned. She had known Quinn a bit over a week, a record time for her to sleep with someone. And that would reflect badly on her, she suspected.

But was she strong enough to keep away from his bed?

The next few days dragged by. The necklace pro-gressed well, even without Quinn's encouraging presence. It was as if all her frustrations poured out into the design. Without consulting him, she altered the model she'd supplied for his approval—that is, his client's approval—and worked fifteen-hour days. Ryan and Jessica's wedding arrangements were well in hand.

Quinn kept to himself and a kind of polite peace enveloped the house.

But by night, it was a different story. Dani was her own worst enemy, reliving their lovemaking over and over. He was a drug she was addicted to. To stop herself from marching into his bedroom, she began justifying his actions. After all, she was being paid an enormous amount of money and an enormous compliment to design a necklace for the most beautiful and valuable stone she was ever likely to see. What did it matter that it was for a client and not him?

And it wasn't like he had tricked her into bed, either. She'd practically ambushed him while he sat at his desk, conducting his business. She couldn't blame him for that.

Had she really expected that something more could come of this "situation" she had rushed headlong into? She was out of his league, not even in the same stratosphere.

One night he told her that Jake Vance's mother had passed away. "The funeral is Friday. Come to Sydney with me and catch up with your family."

She considered it dubiously. "It will put me back on the necklace. I wanted to finish it before the wedding on the twentieth."

"Relax. I'll put it in a bank vault here. I'll charter a flight for Thursday afternoon and we'll return Saturday."

It was the excuse she needed to keep away from him. She went all out for the next few days and made good progress, barely sleeping at all.

And that's probably why she fell asleep on the private plane.

She awoke slowly, fuzzily, dreaming of Quinn, so it was no surprise at all when she saw his face mere inches away. And when he leaned even closer and brushed her mouth with his, she closed her eyes again, didn't even *think* of resisting. After all, that was how the dream was supposed to go. Reliving their lovemaking was how she'd spent every night since the fight.

She stretched toward him, allowed the dream to part her lips, to feel the tip of his tongue seek and find hers. She combed her fingers through his thick hair and her heartbeat quickened and banged loudly in her ears. But she wouldn't open her eyes just yet. She didn't want this to stop, didn't want him to disappear.

His hand moved on her thigh, skimming her silk underskirt over her heated skin. Each stroke lengthened, higher and higher until she shifted restlessly, craving more. Another hand caressed her neck and face as they kissed. The seat belt dug into her hips, making her wriggle against it. Every part of her strained toward him, this faceless lover, this man with his tongue in her mouth, one hand moving down over her blouse to cup and stroke her breast, the other moving ever higher, scorching her thigh. Her arms were trapped against his chest, unable to move far with his weight leaning into her, but she moved toward him, trying to touch him, to inflict some of the same torture on him.

Breathing heavily, he grasped her wrists and stilled her. "Open your eyes, damn it!"

She did and almost quailed at the tortured desire in his. Desire and regret.

Regret for wanting her or for hurting her?

Wide awake now, she gave a shuddering breath, laid her head on the rest and just looked at his face. The heat of passion still smouldered sullenly in the pulse beat on her wrist where he gripped her, and in the aching tips of her breasts and deep inside her centre. But her breathing slowed and she searched his scowling, troubled face, trying to read what he was thinking and feeling.

His breathing had calmed. Gradually the grip on her wrists eased and became more of a caress. He, too, leaned back in his seat facing her, watching her.

Finally his eyes softened and he spoke. "You'll stay with me tonight."

It wasn't a question, or a demand. And—God help her—her heart leapt in her chest with welcome. She'd intended to take a cab to the Blackstone mansion in Vaucluse and surprise her mother. But Dani would take what she could get from Quinn.

Time with him was short and she knew there'd be less of her when their fling ended. The fight had torn them apart physically, and because it was unexpected, the end was hard to accept. Now she had the opportunity to say goodbye properly, make it special. Dani was going to make the most of the day or days she had left with him, and damn the consequences.

They spent the rest of the flight looking at each other. Not kissing now but touching, sweet touches to their hands, cheeks, throat, hair. His eyes burned for her, and that and his touch kept her at a simmer for the remainder of the flight to Sydney, the seemingly endless taxi ride to his building and equally interminable elevator ride to his penthouse apartment.

Giddy with desire, they barely made it inside before he was ripping her clothes off, pushing her up against the wall opposite a massive picture window that showcased beautiful Darling Harbour, Sky Tower, the harbour bridge and the opera house. He took her there and Dani welcomed him into her body and came again and again as the lights of the city swirled behind her eyes like a kaleidoscope on drugs.

Eight

Dani survived the fierce hug and pulled back to survey her mother. "You look…different. Did you get highlights?"

Her mother patted her hair self-consciously while Marcie, the Blackstone housekeeper, bustled around the table.

Sonya Hammond usually wore her brown hair in a neat bun, but today she'd allowed several long spiralling tendrils to escape, giving her a completely different look. Was it her makeup or the unusually colourful teal blouse she'd teamed with smart-looking slacks? Her mother was the epitome of conservative elegance, but today, Dani thought she looked younger somehow, mature-chic. "Have you had a facial or something?"

Sonya ignored her question and instead tsked at

Dani's earrings. "Must your earrings always arrive before you do?"

"I thought these were quite demure." She touched one gold bar with a plaque of smoky quartz on the end. Since she had reinvented herself up in Port Douglas, some of her more bohemian creations stunned her mother, though Sonya was too nice and too fond of Dani's strong sense of individualism to criticise without humour.

"Sit. How is it you're here when we're seeing you in a few days?"

"I told you I was doing a little job for Quinn Everard." Dani leaned forward and sniffed appreciatively at the urn in the middle of the table. "Mmm. Pumpkin soup."

"Yes, I couldn't believe the cheek of the man, after all he's put you through."

The whole family had witnessed the deterioration of Dani's professional reputation at Quinn's hands. Dani tried to ignore the little pang of hurt at her mother's words. "Anyway, he has a funeral to attend today so I came down with him. I need some shoes for the wedding."

"What colour is the dress?" Sonya asked quickly. "No, don't tell me, I'll try to keep an open mind."

Marcie appeared with a soup bowl and a platter of warm Turkish bread and set them down. Her mother looked pointedly at the urn. "Eat up, I have an appointment. Ryan's picking me up any minute."

Dani ladled some soup into her bowl. "I thought you'd want to supervise," she said dryly, "but we can do dinner later and maybe I'll treat you to the movies or something."

Sonya looked uncomfortable. "I can't, dear. I have an engagement. The theatre, actually."

"Oh?" That was unusual. Sonya hardly ever went out in the evenings. She swallowed her soup, watching her mother. New clothes, new hairdo, appointments and engagements… "Who with?"

"Garth, actually."

"How is old Garth?" Dani was relieved. Garth Buick was the Blackstone company secretary and had been ever since Dani could remember. He was probably Howard's closest friend, a nice man, she recalled. A widower for a few years.

"He's not old," her mother said with an edge to her voice. "He's very young and fit."

Dani's spoon stopped halfway to her mouth and the two women locked gazes for a long moment.

Sonya reddened and looked away first. "Close your mouth, Danielle. It's just friendship. He's been teaching me to sail."

"Right," Dani said weakly. "That's great, really."

And it was, she told herself as she slathered butter onto the warm flatbread. Her mother had given her life over to raising her daughter and Howard's kids and then running his household and being his hostess. Whatever Dani's father had done to her, she'd completely withdrawn from relationships outside of the family.

Either that or she'd been walloped with a massive dose of unrequited love. Dani wondered what it would be like to love someone so completely that you never wanted to risk it again.

Was Quinn still in love with his wife? It must be six or seven years since Laura died. Did he still miss her, measure every other woman he met against her? Was Dani about to discover what her mother had all those years ago, that you couldn't compete with a dead woman?

Sonya's smile was resigned. "I can just see your mind ticking over, my girl. Poor old Mum, the dried-up old prune, wasting away for the love of Howard."

Dani shook her head admiringly. How did the woman do it?

"But no," her mother continued. "He was so devastated when Ursula died. I knew then that he would never risk giving his heart completely again. And I didn't intend to be one in a long line of his discarded women."

Clever woman, because that was exactly the way things had turned out. Howard was notorious for his womanising and had never committed to any of them.

Her mother sighed. "I may as well get it over with. My appointment this afternoon is with a real estate agent. I'm looking at a house over in Double Bay."

"But..." Dani was stunned. Her mother leave Miramare? "You have a permanent right to reside in this house." Howard's will stated that.

They both cast their eyes around the room and out to the vista beyond. The first-floor suite Dani had grown up in was much more informal than the rest of the house but still boasted spectacular views of Sydney Harbour and the Pacific Ocean. Sonya combined a love of antiques with a warm, comfortable style of her own. Miramare was a show home, she liked to say, but her suite of rooms was just a home.

Dani could not imagine her mother anywhere else.

"I rattle around here by myself now," Sonya said broodingly. "And what if James Blackstone comes forward? Howard was convinced he was alive or he wouldn't have left the mansion to him in the will."

"This is your home. You are legally entitled. James, if he exists, will just have to accept that." She pushed her plate away, suddenly not hungry. "Besides, what about Marcie?"

"There will always be a place for Marcie. She knows that."

"You've talked about it?" Dani frowned, a little indignant that her mother hadn't shared this with her first.

"I'm just looking, dear," her mother said airily. "When Garth suggested this place was up for sale, I decided to have a peek, that's all."

"Garth suggested… Wait a minute, doesn't Garth live in Double Bay?" Dani didn't know whether to be affronted or delighted, but in the end, delight won out. She couldn't help grinning as her mother fidgeted. It was about time Sonya thought of herself after a lifetime of looking after everyone else.

Sonya cleared her throat. "I'm not moving in with Garth, okay? I'm just looking at a smaller house that happens to be a few blocks from his."

Marcie passed by the table. "I've made up your bed, lovey."

"Oh, I'm not staying."

It was her turn to fidget as two sets of eyes swivelled toward her. "I'm twenty-seven, for crying out loud!"

Marcie scuttled out, grinning.

"Is he as nice-looking as his photo?" Sonya asked.

Dani shrugged. They'd be here all day if she was to outline the myriad ways Quinn Everard appealed to her.

"Do you like him, Danielle?" her mother insisted.

"Would I spend the night with him otherwise?"

Her mother's piercing gaze made her feel about ten years old, as usual. She reconsidered her defensive attitude. It had rarely worked in the past. "I suppose. But he's out of my league."

Sonya raised her aristocratic nose. "Must be hard to walk with that huge chip on your shoulder."

"You haven't met him. He's smooth." *And sometimes rough...* "He owns himself, very self-assured. Supremely comfortable with himself, his place, his ability. And he manages to convey all this without making the minions around him feel inferior." She rolled her eyes ruefully. "Even though it's painfully obvious that's exactly what they are."

Her mother rested her chin on her hand, a faraway look in her eyes. "You do like him," she said softly, and a silence descended as Dani tried and failed to think of a suitable rejoinder.

"Why don't you both come to dinner and the theatre with Garth and me tonight?" her mother asked.

Dani shook her head, somewhat relieved. "He won't be back until late."

"Oh." Sonya looked disappointed. "You, then."

"I'm not playing gooseberry." She was pleased her mother was stepping out but one tiny part of her wanted to think about this for a while. Dani had few enough absolutes in her life already. To think that she may never visit her mother at Miramare again was a sobering thought. "I have heaps to do on this flying visit, honestly," she lied, and decided to change the subject. "You'll never guess who came to visit last week. Matt Hammond."

Sonya's eyes lit up, just as she'd known they would. Dani rummaged through her bag for the photos of Blake that Matt had supplied. Her mother fell on them.

"What's more," Dani added, "he wants me to make him an heirloom necklace from the Blackstone Rose diamonds, though I'm not sure if that's for public consumption just yet."

"I can't believe it! What's he like? Tell me everything!"

"Nice." At least, she had thought so, thought they clicked, but that was now coloured by the conversation she'd overheard. "Really nice."

"You don't sound convinced," her mother said dubiously.

"Oh, I am, it's just that Quinn was there and they were talking business."

The doorbell rang downstairs and Sonya's face fell. "Not now." She grimaced at Dani, obviously wanting to hear more about her nephew. "That'll be Ryan."

"Don't tell him about Matt," Dani whispered.

Ryan looked pleased to see her and they spent a couple of minutes discussing the wedding plans. She was thrilled to see how utterly happy he looked. He and Jessica were expecting twins in a few months. Jessica was blooming, Ryan told her, but worried she'd already outgrown her wedding dress.

"What brings you to Sydney?" Ryan asked.

"I needed special shoes for my dress," she explained.

He rolled his eyes at Sonya. "God help us…."

Dani's fashion sense for these big occasions was legendary. "Don't be mean," she grumbled. "I've gone to a lot of trouble for this wedding. Keeping it quiet has been the hardest thing I've ever done." *Moving into Quinn's house, his bedroom, exploring his body, welcoming his touch…and all just to keep their wedding under wraps.*

Dani smiled, suddenly feeling quite kindly disposed to Ryan Blackstone. "Quinn was coming down for a funeral so I tagged along."

Ryan's brows rose. "Sonya told me you're doing a job for him. I was surprised, given your history."

She shrugged away a pang of hurt. "Client's request."

"Jessica knows Quinn slightly, likes him, I think." His face lapsed into a smile she had never seen on him before. "Still, she likes everyone these days."

Dani's eyes nearly misted over as she witnessed Ryan's happiness. He'd always been a troubled soul. His brother's abduction and mother's suicide were enough of a burden. Add to that the offhand way Howard treated both him and Kimberley, consistently choosing Ric Perrini over Ryan when it came to Blackstone Diamonds. She crossed her fingers under the table and silently wished Ryan all the happiness in the world.

"Who died?" Ryan selected an olive and a slice of cheese from the table. "Quinn's funeral?"

"Jake Vance's mother."

"I'd heard Everard and Vance were chummy. Has

Quinn said anything about Matt Hammond sniffing around?"

Dani shook her head, not looking at Sonya.

"Apparently Hammond was in town last week seeing Vance. The rumour doing the rounds is that Hammond and Vance are out to set up a corporate takeover of Blackstone. Seems Matt's been polling all the shareholders for support."

Sonya opened her mouth. Dani shot her foot out and connected with her mother's ankle. What good would it do for him to know Matt had been in Port talking business with Quinn, too? He'd turned him down.

Sonya prudently said nothing, and she and Ryan dropped Dani at the bus stop for the central city and headed off to their real estate appointment. But even the prospect of shoe shopping did little to quell a growing disquiet. Should she warn the Blackstones about the Jake-Matt-Quinn connection? Was she being disloyal to the family who had provided for her all her life?

She let herself in to Quinn's apartment using the key he had given her. Her feet ached and all she could think about was his large Japanese bath, so it was an unwelcome surprise when the sound of loud voices greeted her.

Four people stood around the island in Quinn's kitchen. A pretty woman with long, tied-back greying hair, looked up first. A tall, lean man stood beside her with one arm draped loosely around her shoulders. Quinn, too, had his arm around someone's shoulders. Someone beautiful, in a lilac suit, with a chic blond bob and striking eyes.

Dani couldn't really take in much more than that.

But then Quinn's eyes beat a path to her face and she felt the energy as if he'd shone an intense spotlight onto her.

"I—I'm sorry," she stammered. "I didn't mean to intrude." God, what must they think? She had his key. "I thought you'd still be out."

Then Quinn dropped his arm from the blonde's shoulders and walked toward her. His eyes shone as he drew her into the circle. There was no mistaking the warmth in his voice as he said, "*This* is Dani," as if he'd been waiting for her to come, dying to introduce her.

As it turned out, this was much better than her anticipated bath. She shook hands with his parents, Gwen and Joseph, and with Lucy, his foster sister, who had the most beautiful, sad violet eyes.

They were ribald and rowdy, and so close, they finished one another's sentences. It was incredible to see Quinn in this light. Outside of the bedroom, his reserve set him apart from everyone; he seemed untouchable. His parents were nothing like that, and when he was with them, neither was he. There was so much warmth, humour and concern for one another in this kitchen. She loved her mother dearly but she'd never stood around a kitchen counter with her family members, drinking, joking and sharing memories.

Yes, it was a sad day for the Everards, but as often happens with funerals, the relief of getting through it sometimes manifests itself in a need to drink. "Especially when you're Irish!" Joseph intoned, holding out his glass for a top-up, while Quinn shook his head at her, mouthing, "He's not Irish."

Dani thought back to the tensions that had accompanied Howard's funeral; the reserve, the constant media crush, everyone watching one another to make sure they didn't fall apart, or wondering who knew what about Howard's eventful life.

That all seemed a million miles away. Corporate takeovers, too, seemed a million miles away. She swapped blueberry muffin recipes with Gwen, had an eye-popping dance with Joseph to a Leonard Cohen song, and Lucy confided she had discovered Dani's knickers under the couch.

"Must be his other girlfriend," Dani told her. "I never wear them."

"I don't think so." Lucy laughed. "Quinn *never* invites a woman to stay over here."

Everyone left a couple of hours later and Quinn ordered in pasta, which they ate in his tub. She lay across from him as he struggled to keep his eyes open, and cautioned herself to guard her heart. Her expectations of people were too high. A throwaway remark by Lucy, the warmth in his eyes when she crashed their party...there was danger in allowing herself to hope she could ever be admitted to the circle of love she had just glimpsed.

Her fingers swirled the water in front of her, making a whirlpool, and Dani recognised she was in an uncontrolled spiral. She was falling in love, and not only with Quinn, but with the idea of his family, too.

Quinn came into his living room to see Dani standing in front of the window looking out at Sydney's skyline, her bag by her feet.

Yes, he thought. He'd wanted her here, to see what she looked like, see if she'd fit. And if that hadn't prompted him to take a swan dive off the balcony, then he was going to try her out on his parents. Only they had preempted that by inviting themselves over last night.

And hadn't that gone well?

The polite tension of the past few days in Port Douglas had made him miserable. Being relegated from lover to boss shouldn't have bothered a man who, since Laura's death, hadn't considered forever. At thirty-four years old, Quinn had never wondered till now whether he was missing out on anything.

He hadn't expected to enjoy her so much.

Dani turned and smiled at him and he gave himself a mental shake. "All packed?"

What the next step was, he couldn't be sure, but Quinn knew one thing. Where Dani Hammond was concerned, he was at least prepared to admit that there would be a next step.

She nodded and reached for her bag, just as Quinn's phone rang. It was Sir John Knowles, former prime minister, outgoing governor-general, and close friend and mentor of Quinn's. A call he had to take.

He walked into his office and after very little preamble, Sir John got to the point of his call. Incredulous, Quinn listened to the man's earth-shattering admission, and in seconds the feeling of peace Quinn had woken with was ground to dust.

"Taxi's here." Dani stood at the doorway to his office, holding her bag.

Quinn covered the mouthpiece of his phone. "I have to take this. You go on and I'll meet you at the airstrip."

She left and he returned to his phone call. Based on Sir John's admission, Quinn had no alternative.

"I want out, John."

The older man's quiet voice begged him. How could he turn him down?

"I've become personally involved. I won't lie about something like this."

"Please, Quinn, just another few days. I wouldn't ask this of you if it wasn't the last chance I have."

"Allow *me* to tell her, then."

"I can't risk her refusal, don't you see? And I haven't told Clare yet. Not about the prognosis or the other."

The old man sounded sick and alone. His last chance. Quinn had heard that before, had lived with his failure for seven years.

But still, it was a lousy thing to do. "You don't know what you're asking."

"I do, believe me. And I wouldn't ask it of anyone but you, because I know you won't let me down."

"Quinn, will you come to the wedding with me?"

He sat back in his chair and displayed the same careful expression he'd had since they got back from Sydney three days ago.

Dani was worried. The rumours Ryan spoke of in Sydney had now been aired on television. The shareholders of Blackstone Diamonds were restless, despite an assurance from Kimberley in the paper this morning that all was well.

Perhaps if he knew the Blackstones, was personally involved, he wouldn't be so hasty to offer his support to Matt.

Quinn set his pen down. "That's not a good idea," he said slowly.

"Why not?"

"It's a family occasion. With the events of the past few months, everyone will be feeling a little nostalgic." He looked at her steadily. "My history with Howard is bound to raise comment. I don't want to rub everyone's nose in it."

"I don't think anyone will—"

"I'll let you know if I change my mind, okay?" He picked up his pen again, his eyes unreadable. "How's the necklace coming along?"

"Okay." The client had imposed a deadline for completion—the twenty-fifth. She was on track, Dani thought, assuming she kept her mind on the job instead of wondering what Quinn Everard was up to.

Nine

"Look who I found on the doorstep." Dani was on her way out to collect various members of the Blackstone clan from the airport when Jake Vance's face appeared before her. She left the guest with Quinn, gave her apologies and rushed out to her task.

Quinn's smile faded at his friend's grim expression. What was up? Jake kept a brutal schedule. He didn't just show up on a whim.

Quinn waved Jake into a seat. "Coffee?"

"You have something stronger?"

Quinn narrowed his gaze but held up a bottle of cognac.

"My old mate Hennessey." Jake nodded gratefully.

Quinn poured two generous snifters.

"No wonder you're AWOL." Jake's head gestured to the door where Dani had just left. "Well, more AWOL than usual."

Quinn stayed silent and sipped his drink, waiting for Jake to come to the point.

The silence stretched, then Jake leaned forward and placed his glass on Quinn's desk. "Sounds important."

"I didn't say a word," Quinn retorted, exasperated.

"Exactly," Jake said smugly. "Not often you have a girl stay over at your apartment."

"How did you…?"

"Lucy."

"You and Lucy are talking?" Quinn leaned forward, arms folded on the desk.

"Don't get excited. She called the day after the funeral, before she headed off back to England. Just a friendly take-care-of-yourself call."

"She was worried you wouldn't want her at the funeral," Quinn mused. Jake was ripped to shreds when Lucy left him after several years together. Quinn tried not to take sides and loved both of them, but he never wanted to see that hurt inflicted on either of them again.

Jake shrugged. "I appreciated it."

"What brings you up here? Bottom fallen out of the market?" Quinn hoped it was nothing to do with Matt Hammond and his Blackstone Diamond shares. He didn't need any more secrets upsetting the applecart with Dani.

Jake took a healthy gulp of liquor, screwing up his face. "In a roundabout way, it concerns the little lady who just rushed out of here with her tail on fire." He fixed Quinn a stern look. "Drink up. This is going to come as a shock."

Quinn listened in disbelief as his closest friend related how his mother, shortly before she died, told him he was not her birth child. She'd found him as a two-year-old at the site of a fatal car accident. The car had been washed into a river and the two other occupants were dead.

Jake rubbed his eyes wearily. "I thought she was delirious. And when she insisted that I was Howard Blackstone's son, I was sure she was delirious."

Quinn's eyes felt like saucers. He raised his hand. "Back up. This was before she died?"

"I didn't mention it at the funeral because…well, I just didn't believe it. But I've been going through the house." He opened the briefcase he'd laid on the other chair and took out a large scrapbook. "It's all in there, Quinn." He patted the book. "God Almighty, I've never been so scared in my life."

Quinn rose with the bottle and walked around the desk to top up Jake's glass. He perched on the edge of the desk and put out his hand for the scrapbook.

Jake kept talking as Quinn flipped the pages.

"How I was kidnapped as a toddler by the housekeeper and her boyfriend. How they sent a ransom note and Howard did all he could to get me back, but on the way to pick up the money, the car crashed."

Quinn glanced at him periodically while reading the newspaper clippings. He tried to imagine the dark-haired little boy in the photos as a grown man, even as his rational mind rejected the notion. He glanced up at Jake's dark green eyes, coal-black hair and at the fully formed widow's peak—as opposed to just a hint of one in the baby photos.

"My mother happened on the accident and it all went a bit haywire. She'd lost a baby the year before to SIDS and was on the run from her deadbeat boyfriend. She was going somewhere where no one knew her. Anyway, she was probably a little crazy at the time—hormones, grief, whatever—so she picked me up and passed me off as her own."

Quinn got to the last page and snapped the book shut. The dates could work, though it would make Jake a year older. It must be true, or else a very elaborate hoax, but why would April, Jake's mother, lie at the end when she had nothing to lose?

"My God," he breathed. "You're a Blackstone."

"I'm *not* a Blackstone!" Jake countered, then he put his face in his hands. "What the hell am I going to do now?"

They talked and drank all afternoon. Quinn suggested a DNA test to eliminate April as his birth mother.

"Already done it," Jake said. "The results should be through in a few days."

They agreed he should talk to his lawyers and accountants. It was common knowledge that Howard Blackstone's amended will instructed a six-month delay of disbursements pertaining to James while his whereabouts were investigated. Jake thought April's ex-husband, Bill Kellerman, must have got wind of the investigation and threatened her, so she decided to forewarn him.

The living Blackstones were not likely to welcome him with open arms. Matt Hammond's intention to stir things up in the Blackstone boardroom was another complication. "You'll need Matt onside in case they turn on you," Quinn warned. "And watch your back. Ryan and Ric Perrini are chips off the old block. Don't trust anyone. The Blackstones have a leak somewhere in their organisation." That much he knew. Someone close to the Blackstones was providing little snippets of information to those in the industry. That was how Quinn had stumbled onto Ryan and Jessica's wedding plans.

When Dani arrived home a while later, she popped her head in the office to ask if they wanted coffee. Though they both probably needed coffee by this point, judging by the depleted brandy bottle, they declined.

"Don't worry," Quinn reassured his friend when he saw him staring after Dani. "I'll keep it quiet."

Jake turned his head to look at him. "You serious about her?"

The million-dollar question, Quinn thought, leaning back and folding his arms. "Define *serious*."

"I couldn't define squat at the moment."

Quinn had given considerable thought to the question but was little closer to an answer. At his mother's funeral, Jake had spoken of the importance of family, which made Quinn think of the relationships that were vital to him. He was as proud of Lucy, who'd dragged herself up from nothing, as if she were his real sister. Watching Jake grow into the confident, successful business baron he was had been one of Quinn's greatest pleasures in life, and he had no qualms that however upsetting the situation with the Blackstones became, Jake would face it squarely and prevail. Even his parents were constantly motivated to change things for the better. They were now busy fund-raising for a caravan to take to the inner-city streets as a drop-in centre for the street kids of Newtown.

Quinn loved them all and was proud to share in their successes, but sharing was nothing new for him. He'd grown up sharing everything until Laura died— and then he had nothing left. He'd closed himself off, kept his motor idling, but somehow had stalled here in Port Douglas.

He was passionate about his work, hugely success- ful, but he did have to question whether or not he was growing. Because from where he sat, he was doing the same things he was five years ago, while everyone else had moved on.

Quinn stared at a point somewhere above his friend's shoulder. "I've always felt it was unfair to ask a woman to sit around waiting while I'm off travelling the globe."

"Liar!" scoffed Jake. "You've never even *considered* asking a woman to sit around waiting for you."

Quinn grinned and picked up his glass. He made a thoughtful study of his friend through the amber liquid. "There's this woman I know in Milan. I see her every three or four months for one or two nights. I like her, but we both know that's all it is, a one-night stand every so often. I remember her birthday, I buy her nice things, take her out somewhere nice…." He emptied his glass in one swallow, grimacing at the burn. "But that's all there is. I was happy with that, damn it!"

"About time." Jake stood and approached the desk, tipping the bottle up to empty the last drops into Quinn's glass.

"You can talk!" he retorted. His grin faded. "She's like no one else. Every minute with her is a keeper. Suddenly, my life, which I've always thoroughly enjoyed—"

"Stinks!" Jake nodded sympathetically.

"No!" Quinn drained his glass and his eyes watered. "It just seems a bit lame, that's all."

After he poured Jake into a cab and sent him off to the airport, Quinn went to find Dani, nursing a moderate headache from the effects of the brandy. She lay mostly submerged in a bath full of fragrant bubbles, chewing her nails. He tapped her hand away, admonishing her. "You going out, I suppose?"

She nodded. "I didn't think you would want to come."

Quinn sat on the edge of the bath, the steam and the brandy fuzzing his brain. He most certainly didn't want to spend the evening with the Blackstones.

Then again, maybe it would help Jake to know something of the family dynamics. Who was top dog, who was most likely to oppose his appearance, and who—if anyone—might offer the hand of friendship.

An idea was forming....

"Quinn, have you told anyone about the wedding?"

He squinted at her. Her hair was mostly piled up on top of her head, a long coiled strand clinging to her damp shoulder. "Nope." He reached out and tugged the curl gently, straightening it. It bounced back when he let it go.

"It's just, I know Port Douglas, and there's something going on. I can smell a press photographer a mile off."

He blinked as her words sunk into his brain. "You think *I* tipped off the press?"

She reached out and touched his knee, leaving a wet

patch, but Quinn's indignation faded fast when her movement stirred up the bubbles and a very pink and pert nipple peeped out of the froth.

"No," she answered. "I just think there's something going on, something not quite right."

He bit back the words before they tumbled from his mouth. *"With us, you mean?"* Where the hell had that thought come from? Whatever he did, he could not get into a deep and meaningful conversation after half a bottle of cognac. He dipped his hand into the steaming water and rubbed his face. "I probably deserve suspicion." After all, he had blackmailed her about the wedding in the first place.

When you thought about it, he deserved to be hung, drawn and quartered for all the lies he'd told, all the secrets he withheld. Layer upon layer of secrets. Just when he'd decided he might take a chance on her, look ahead a little— *kapow!* And then *kapow* again. First Sir John, and now Jake. What next? And however could he justify it to her?

She looked up at him thoughtfully. "I didn't think you would contact the media. I just…" She sighed and reached to the side for a sponge, her knee bending up out of the water. "I just so want this day to be perfect for Ryan and Jessica."

Perfect? Quinn knew what was perfect. A smooth pink knee foaming with bubbles. He felt hard as a rock suddenly and licked his dry lips. "Jake," he croaked. "The press will be after Jake."

She looked up at him, a relieved smile forming on her delectable mouth. "You think?"

"He attracts attention wherever he goes. You planning on finishing that?" He nodded at the sponge resting on her knee. The thought of it was attracting all sorts of attention in all sorts of places.

"What was he doing here, anyway?"

Quinn reached out and took the sponge from her hand, his fingers digging into its soft porous depths. "Business. Lift your leg."

"My leg?" Dani hesitated, probably expecting a more expansive reply to her question about Jake's unexpected visit.

Quinn's eyes shifted to hers, challenging her. He had business in mind, all right. Funny business.

And he didn't want any more questions—or any more guilt.

Holding her gaze, he moved his hand into the water and soaked the sponge. Sultry understanding glowed in her eyes. Forget Jake. A trickle of steamy sweat slid down his temple. Forget Blackstone and the press and the shares. Forget life-altering secrets. The swish of streaming water filled his ears as her shapely, heat-flushed thigh rose up from the foam, and then her calf and foot flexed prettily. Quinn caught hold of her foot, washing it while she squirmed.

He cleared his throat. "I've been thinking, may I change my mind and come to the wedding, after all?"

The little smile that curved her lips warmed him. "I'd like that," she said slowly, watching as he dipped the sponge and stretched her leg out. "I'll set it up tonight," she promised.

Quinn stroked the back of her calf and thigh with the

sponge. Water dripped down his forearms and onto his thighs and he thought he must be one sick unit because the warmth and wetness of it only fuelled his desire more.

"Exactly how long do I have to get you clean before you go out?"

Ten

The day of the wedding had finally arrived.

Quinn knocked on her door to say the car was here. Dani was on edge, swimming in questions. Would he like her dress? Would her family like him, and vice versa? What was Jake doing up here? Why were the media swarming all over town, sipping coffee in the cafés, propping up the bars everywhere she turned?

And Quinn's sudden turnaround about accompanying her to the wedding. What was that about?

She made a final adjustment to the chiffon scarf she had cleverly twisted into her long French knot, picked up her purse and joined Quinn downstairs, loving the light in his eyes as he watched her descend.

And would he leave for good once she finished the necklace? Dani worried about that most of all.

They were driven to a helicopter port and, minutes later, were lifted up and over the rain forest to a beach just a few miles south. Dani had inspected the premises previously but was unprepared for the beauty of the place from the air.

The entire van Berhopt Resort hovered above an unsurpassed vista of rain forest and sea. Built on a raised knoll, the lodge appeared to be suspended over the secluded beach below, like a bird about to launch into the air. With a body of glass and steel, somehow it merged with the surroundings, complementing the bird's-eye view. For one breathless moment, Dani thought they were going to land on the massive curved roof that arced above the building, its eaves on all sides overhanging and imposing.

"Spectacular!" Quinn breathed in her ear as the helicopter thankfully set down a couple of hundred metres away from the lodge.

Dani could imagine the reaction of the wedding guests as they were flown in pairs to this incredible secluded paradise. Golf carts took them up to the house. The reception was to start at four-thirty with cocktails and nibbles, then the marriage ceremony. Afterward, there was a sumptuous buffet, featuring the best the tropical north could offer. Only the bride and groom would stay the night here, with the guests being ferried back to their hotels in Port by limousines. It was a small gathering of only twenty family and friends.

In his platinum tux and mahogany-and-silver-striped tie, Quinn Everard was the perfect escort for a tropical, late-afternoon wedding, sophisticated and breathtakingly handsome. His cool against her flamboyance. Dani proudly took his arm and walked through the lobby out to the pool area where the guests were already gathered. Ryan and Jessica had arrived first to settle into their suite. Several other couples lounged around the pool, being served by white-jacketed waiters with silver trays that glinted off the blue water. Dani waved at Sonya and Garth on the other side of the pool and prepared to present Quinn to Ryan Blackstone.

"Well, well," said Ryan as they approached. "Quinn Everard, I presume." He held out his hand. "Welcome to the lion's den."

Quinn smiled and took the proffered hand. "Congratulations, Ryan. It's a pleasure to be here."

Jessica offered Quinn her cheek. "How lovely to see you, Quinn."

"Jessica, you look stunning."

And she did. The bride glowed in a jewel-encrusted champagne gown, a stunning clasp of rose-gold and pink diamonds in between her breasts. "A gift from Ryan," she whispered to Dani, who was so taken with the brooch, she instinctively reached out and touched her fingertips to it. The lovely gown flattered her rounded belly and no amount of sparkle could eclipse the proud smile on Jessica's face or the warmth in her beautiful brown eyes.

While Quinn and Ryan chose drinks from a tray, Jessica turned to Dani and hugged her. "I can't thank you enough for all you've done. This place just takes my breath away."

"I thought you'd like it."

"Everything is just perfect, Danielle. The setting, the weather, the menu you chose and, oh my God, the suite! I don't intend moving out of there for a week!"

The bride took Dani's arm and walked a few steps away. "You look positively beautiful. That colour has no right looking so sensational with your hair…"

Dani expected a few raised brows about her dress, especially from her mother. Strapless and backless, the fabric was hummer orange but the chiffon overskirt was made up of thousands of tiny overlapping patches of deep pink blush and vivid orange. When she moved, the patches rippled with the richness of the sunset.

"You and Quinn look cosy together."

Dani smiled. "I appreciate his invitation at such short notice."

Jessica nodded and sipped her orange juice. "I've met him socially a few times at launches and jewellery expos. He's charming and knows his stuff. And more handsome than any man has a right to be."

Dani helped herself to a delicious morsel from a platter offered her by a server, thinking she wasn't going to argue with Jessica's assessment.

Her soon-to-be cousin-in-law eyed her speculatively. "Is this part of the job description or likely to grow into a more permanent position?"

"I think I'll keep our positions to myself for the moment, Bridezilla." She stopped, her smile fading, and stared across the pool. "Would you look at that?"

Her mother and Garth were putting on a display for Kim and another couple she didn't know. Dani realised it was quite a well-rehearsed tango.

"Did Sonya tell you they were taking lessons together?"

"No. She mentioned sailing." Dani sipped her champagne. "They look good together."

"They *are* good together," Jessica murmured.

Dani felt a twinge of regret that she wasn't in the loop when it looked like this relationship was already quite advanced. But she shook it off. Her mother had never looked better and Dani was thrilled for her. It would just take a bit of getting used to. "Only last week she fobbed me off with the 'just friends' bulldust."

Dani moved to Quinn's side and slid her arm through his. "Let's go say hi to my mother before she dances into the pool and is swept out to sea."

Quinn and Sonya hit it off immediately, and Garth, the Blackstone company secretary and long-time friend and confidant of Howard's, showed no sign of any residual prejudice toward Quinn. Kimberley also greeted him warmly and Dani learned that they had met before in the diamond houses of Europe.

She sensed a slightly cooler dynamic from Ric Perrini toward her escort throughout the evening. She couldn't put her finger on it so decided not to worry about it, wanting nothing to spoil the beautiful wedding she'd helped arrange.

Ryan and Jessica became man and wife as the sun slid beneath the rain forest behind them, setting the sea in front ablaze with light. As if on cue, cockatoo and fruit bats set up their dusk chorus. It was a beautiful ceremony with a stunning backdrop, and there was barely a dry female eye in the place.

Afterward, everyone filled their plates from an amazing buffet of mud crab, ostrich, the local barramundi fish, and many other delicacies popular in this part of the country. The long table accommodated everyone and sat above the pool and the terraced grounds leading to the white sand beach. Jessica announced that the guests should sit next to someone different with each course. Dani knew everyone except a couple of school friends of the bride and her parents. Jessica's father was in a wheelchair but he didn't let it slow him down at all, and his wife and daughter were very attentive.

Sonya whispered that she was seriously considering making an offer on the house she and Ryan had viewed. Her mother living elsewhere than Miramare meant the end of an era was under way. Dani may not have known her father, but at least she'd had a family home, of sorts.

But there was a freshness and vitality to Sonya that Dani couldn't remember seeing before. Her life had been mapped out so young with a child of her own and the responsibility of Kim and Ryan. It gladdened Dani to think her mother was finally going to live a little.

At the next switch, she chatted to Jarrod Hammond and his beautiful fiancée, Briana. The handsome lawyer seemed very much at ease given the bad blood between the two families. Over dessert, she told him how pleased she was to see Matt in Port Douglas a couple of weeks ago. "He hinted that we might all get together soon, Blake, too."

"Great news." Jarrod sounded enthusiastic and

turned to Briana. "We'd be happy to host some sort of gathering in Melbourne, if that suits everyone."

Briana nodded enthusiastically and then responded to the bride's summons at the other end of the table.

Dani looked to where Sonya was deep in conversation with Garth. "Mum can't wait to meet him."

"Meet who?" Ric Perrini, resplendent in white, sat down in Briana's seat.

Dani liked Ric immensely. No one was more thrilled than she when he and Kimberley remarried last month. Despite their long separation, and the fact that relations were not always warm between Ric and Ryan, he was as much a part of the family as she was, in her mind. He'd stuck up for her over moving up here after the humiliation of her broken engagement. She was especially grateful for the support he'd been to Sonya in the past difficult months, and for bringing Kimberley home where she belonged.

"Matt Hammond," she answered. "He came to see me last week."

Ric's eyes shot to her face. "Here?"

She nodded, suddenly unwilling to mention her latest commission. Matt hadn't asked her to keep the Bridal Rose necklace a secret, but the Blackstones could not be expected to applaud the stripping of Howard's legacy and name from the famous pink diamonds. Dani wanted nothing to spoil this night.

"And what," Ric asked, glancing at Jarrod, "would Matt want to see you about, little one?"

Dani often felt like Ric's little sister. "Business of course, old man."

Ric's blue eyes sparkled. "You being such a hot businesswoman, Danielle," he quipped, "Hammond better watch out he doesn't lose his shirt."

Dani was distracted by a slight tension to Jarrod's jaw. Would this stupid feud ever disappear? Sure, it was decades in the making, but why did the younger generation continue to suffer? She turned back to Ric. "Not me, silly. Quinn."

"You called?"

Quinn's sleeve brushed her bare shoulder as he leaned over her to set his dessert plate down.

"Ryan wants a word," he said quietly. His breath trickled into her ear, reminding her of how she loved his voice and how much she had missed hearing it for the past hour. Closing her eyes, she leaned slightly back into him and inhaled, familiarising herself with his warmth and bulk and the unique scent of him that made her feel most like a woman. His woman.

Reluctantly she looked up the table to where the bridegroom stood talking to the manager of the lodge. Ryan's grim expression told her something was wrong. "Problem?" she whispered to Quinn, rising.

"Could be." Quinn put his hand on the small of her back and they walked up the length of the table.

"There's a reporter at the reception desk wanting confirmation of our wedding," Ryan said tightly. "I really don't want this to become a circus." He glanced to where his bride sat with her parents and Kimberley, looking for all the world like she didn't have a care.

"I'll go and talk to him," Dani began.

"I'll go," Quinn said quickly. "If he's from Sydney,

he'll know your face and that you're connected to the Blackstones. The vultures won't think for a minute I would be invited to a Blackstone wedding."

Ryan and Dani nodded, seeing the sense in that. "What will you say?"

"That I'm entertaining important clients from overseas. We're staying the night and will be leaving first thing in the morning. That way, hopefully your honeymoon will go undetected."

"Do you trust him, Danielle?" Ryan asked as they watched him follow the manager out to the reception desk.

She nodded, but unbidden, his threat to reveal the wedding plans to the media on the day they met pressed down on her like a grey cloud. "Don't worry." She squeezed Ryan's arm, swallowing her concerns. "Quinn is the soul of discretion. Nothing is going to spoil the night."

Two hours later, it seemed she was right. The champagne flowed and the party had become quite lively. Finally the bride and groom announced they were retiring to get started on their wedding night. One by one, white stretch limos pulled up to the lobby and the guests piled in and were treated to more champagne they didn't need on the way back to Port Douglas.

Dani and Quinn joined Ric and Kimberley in the back of the last car. Ric, still smarting from the media scrum at his Sydney harbour wedding six weeks before, thanked Quinn for getting rid of the press. "How the hell did they find out? I swear, when I discover who is keeping tabs on our family…"

"I'm starting to think it's someone in the office,"

Kimberley said thoughtfully. "There have been too many coincidences lately."

Dani felt pleasantly tired and snuggled into Quinn's side. "Quinn thinks the press are in town because Jake was here yesterday."

"Jake Vance?" Ric lifted his head. "What was he doing here?"

"He came to see Quinn," she replied. "They're friends."

The atmosphere in the limo chilled. In the dim interior, she saw Ric's nostrils flare and Kim's forehead crease with consternation.

Ric exchanged glances with his wife. "You've had a busy week, Quinn. First Matt Hammond, now Jake Vance." His fingers rasped over his chin. "Somebody is buying up a whole lot of Blackstone shares. You know anything about that?"

There was a long silence while Dani kicked herself for making the inadvertent comment.

"I might," Quinn said eventually. "What of it?"

"I knew it!" Ric said through gritted teeth. "I knew Matt Hammond was involved."

Kimberley put a hand on his arm, but Ric leaned forward and fixed Quinn with a piercing stare. "Hammond's called on both you and Vance in the past week or so. Do you expect me to believe you didn't discuss your Blackstone shareholding?"

"You can believe what you like. You know we're all shareholders. And for the moment, I'm happy with the status quo." Then Quinn, too, leaned forward, bringing his face close to Ric's. "And that's all I'm going to say about that."

His tone was dangerously low and loaded with warning. The two men eyeballed each other while Dani and Kim exchanged worried glances.

"I don't trust you, Everard," Ric said softly.

"Why should you?"

"Are you using Danielle to get an in with the family?"

"Ric!" Dani and Kimberley protested together.

"Watch your mouth," Quinn murmured.

The hairs on the back of Dani's neck rose. Danger throbbed in the air between the two men. Quinn pressed forward and slightly into her side, as if to shield her.

"Can you honestly tell me that you three are not plotting a takeover of Blackstone Diamonds?" Ric's voice was equally low, equally full of threat. "It's a reasonable request, Quinn."

"It's an unreasonable request," Quinn said evenly. "And I'm not privy to Matt's business dealings. But I'm happy with my minor shareholding." His chin rose. "At the moment."

Ric's eyes narrowed but he sat fractionally back, a little of the tension leaving his face. "And Vance?"

"What of him?"

"What's he been meeting with Matt about in Sydney?"

"Jake's business is his own…but I think he has other things on his mind right now."

"Jake's mother just passed away," Dani supplied in a small voice.

"But if he asked for your support?" Ric wasn't letting it go just yet.

Quinn paused while Dani held her breath.

"If he asked," Quinn said heavily, "I would support him."

Ric inhaled, glaring, but Kim beat him to it. She dipped her dark head between them and fixed both men with a formidable look. "That's enough! It's a happy day, damn it!"

Eleven

The car dropped Kim and Ric off at their hotel in town and set off for Four Mile. The tension remained, waves of it, and Dani and Quinn barely spoke. At least the actual wedding had gone off without a hitch, but the argument in the car had raised a barrage of questions that only Quinn could answer. Maybe because of the way they met, she would always have these reservations about him. That was a sobering thought.

They got out of the car and she stopped him from going inside. "We need to talk. Let's go out on the beach."

"You'll ruin your dress."

She shrugged and walked to the end of the road and the copse of trees that led out onto the sand. "I think better out here." She looked back at him. "And you have to tell the truth on my beach. It's my special place."

She was glad he didn't argue. The cover of darkness and the sound of the waves eased her nerves, which would help her ask the questions she needed to. Right now, she was more afraid than she had ever been in her life.

They walked slowly, aimlessly, onto the soft, thick sand. Dani slipped her sandals off, picked them up and turned to face him, her heart in her mouth. "Quinn, I want to know that you're not plotting to bring down Blackstone Diamonds."

He stood very still, looking at her for such a long time that she thought he wasn't going to answer. Would he cut her down again, tell her she had no right to question him? In the darkness, his eyes were unreadable.

Finally he spoke. "To tell you would be to betray a confidence."

She licked her dry lips. "I won't betray your confidence, but I need to know I mean more to you than a few shares."

Quinn inhaled deeply, his chest rising, his eyes boring into her. The silence stretched between them, and again she almost lost hope that he would speak.

She began to turn away, burning with humiliation.

Quinn reached out and caught her hand. "It's Jake. It's about Jake."

Her heart sank further. So Jake Vance *was* planning a corporate takeover, and Quinn had decided to be involved. Ric's words in the car—*Are you using Danielle to get an in with the family?*—returned to taunt her.

When was someone ever going to want her for her?

A full moon broke through the heavy cloud above, bathing everything in an eerie bluish-grey light.

"He…" Quinn's head rolled back and he sighed heavily. "There's no easy way to say this. Jake has reason to believe he is James Hammond Blackstone."

Dani jerked, staring at him stupidly. "Sorry?"

Quinn repeated himself.

Her reservations fled. That was the last thing she'd expected. "Doesn't he know who he is?"

"He thought he did."

"I don't believe it."

"He doesn't, either. That's why he's getting a DNA test done to prove that April—his mother—is his birth mother."

Her hand slid out of his. "He told you this yesterday? That's why he came?"

"It was the first I'd heard of it." Quinn nodded. He proceeded to give her the rundown on Jake's version of events.

"Jake didn't believe her. She was on morphine at that stage, and he thought her mind was going. But when he was packing up the house, he found a scrapbook and it's all there, Dani. Dozens of news clippings about the kidnapping and the housekeeper and her partner who took him. Toys and a blanket from the car that matched what was taken from James Blackstone's bedroom."

Dani's shoulder rose and fell in a helpless movement. "You're telling me this woman, this April, goes to the store one day and comes home with a baby and no one thinks anything of it?" She laughed disbelievingly. "That was big news back then, Quinn, all over Australia. She'd never have gotten away with it."

"He's still looking into it, but it appears that April had a baby who died the year before. At the time she found

Jake—James—she was running away from an abusive boyfriend. She moved around a lot and ended up in South Australia, where no one knew her." He exhaled and looked down, moving his shoe over a sandy mound of crab balls. "I knew April. She had her faults, mostly due to the men she hooked up with, but she was a decent woman. And she loved Jake. There was never any doubt about that."

Dani clasped her hands in front of her and rocked on her heels, sinking into the cool sand. "Oh Lord, this is really going to… So he's not trying to destroy Blackstone Diamonds, after all?" She gave another short sharp laugh. "In fact, that would be counter-productive since he is now the heir."

"Maybe," he warned. "Not confirmed yet."

In a tiny way, although this was earth-shattering news, Dani was a bit relieved. At least he wasn't plotting to bring about the downfall of her cousins. "So why did you suddenly change your mind about coming to the wedding?"

"I wanted to see everyone together, how they all get on, and who Jake's greatest opponent might be when—if—it all comes out." He exhaled. "I think we've established that."

She realised he meant Ric. "If Jake really is family, Ric'll accept it. If he does anything to hurt the company, that's a different matter. It's Kimberley and Ryan—especially Ryan—I'm worried about." Dani turned, rubbing her arms. Quinn slipped off his jacket and placed it around her shoulders and they began to walk slowly back the way they'd come. "I have to tell them."

Quinn inhaled sharply. "No!"

"Quinn, this is too—"

He grasped her arm firmly, turning her. "He won't get the results of April's DNA till next week. If that confirms that April is not his birth mother, then he is going to have to persuade Kim or Ryan, or both, to take a DNA test to prove Howard and your aunt were his parents."

Good luck with that, she thought, imagining Ryan's response to that request. "Quinn, I can't keep something like this from them. It's not fair."

Quinn smiled tightly. "Who said life is fair? Dani, there is a leak in the Blackstone offices. Kimberley said as much tonight. Do you realise the media frenzy something like this will generate? You have to keep it quiet until it's proved that April is not his birth mother." His eyes were grim. "Don't even tell your mother. Garth could be the leak, for all we know."

"Garth? He wouldn't!"

"Probably not. But there is no sense upsetting everyone till we know for sure."

Dani pulled the sides of his jacket closer, chilled by the realisation that on top of all this upset, there would be publicity. Lots of publicity. "God, I hate secrets. I can't even imagine what this is going to do to the family, after the year we've had."

"If it turns out that he really is part of the family, then that's a good thing for everyone, right?"

"Possibly." Possibly not. "Families aren't my strong point. Perhaps I have a jaundiced view." She raised her hand, nibbling on a fingernail. "How would you feel if it was your long-lost brother?"

Quinn considered. "Family's family to me," he said thoughtfully, pulling her hand away from her mouth. "But I suppose if a complete stranger suddenly appeared and wanted to take over the reins of all I'd worked for…" He held his palm up when she began to speak. "And just remember, it was Howard who changed his will to include James, it wasn't Jake's idea."

"Poor old Howard," Dani murmured with genuine sympathy for the man who had never given up hope. "He died before seeing his dream come true."

Quinn nodded. "It must be tough to lose a child."

Dani had her own views on that. "Not for everybody." Her own father had never looked back. She put a hand on his shoulder and raised a foot to slide her sandal back on.

Quinn took the remaining shoe from her hand and bent to put it on her foot. He remained squatting, peering up at her. His face was in shadow, the moon behind him. "Aren't you the least bit curious about your own father? Don't you want to know who and why?"

She looked at him sharply, wondering how the heck he'd known what was going through her mind. "Why should I? He's never been curious about me."

Even as the words left her mouth, she knew she was lying. She'd begged and cajoled, but her mother wouldn't be moved on that subject. *"Forget him, Danielle. He didn't want us and we're better off without him."* She wouldn't even confirm or deny if he was actually still alive.

Quinn slowly rose to his feet. "What if you found out that it wasn't his fault, wasn't his idea to stay away?"

"Then he is a lame excuse for a man," she declared.

What kind of a man made no phone calls, sent no birthday cards—not even once. Even if her mother hated him, it was no excuse to ignore his child. "He never gave a damn, end of story."

She cringed at the tight, self-pitying tone of her voice and turned and walked toward the house.

"You know, there is something my parents and Laura did with some of the kids at home," Quinn said from behind her, and she slowed to let him catch up. "Many of them hadn't seen or spoken to their parents in years. Many had been abused or beaten or just ignored. They used to say, 'If you had the chance, if your mother or father was standing here right now, what would you say to them?'"

Dani hesitated. "I wouldn't say anything. He means nothing to me."

Quinn caught her hand and turned her to face him. "If he was here, right now, Dani, and prepared to listen…?"

With a moody sigh, Dani looked past him, down to the waves lapping the sand. What would she say, indeed? She stared into nothing and tried to imagine what he looked like, this make-believe father. Would he be tall, have red hair like hers? A kindly face?

She could stare into nothing all she liked. There were no answers there. She'd already looked, many, many times.

"I'd say 'you're late.'" She looked into Quinn's face. "I'd say 'you're too bloody late!'"

The next day, they met Sonya for brunch at her hotel before the Blackstones took off for Sydney in the company jet. Her mother knew nothing of the argument in the car the night before with Ric, and Dani did not intend to enlighten her. Besides, the bombshell about Jake was the overriding topic in her mind.

During the meal, a reporter stopped by the table to ask for confirmation of Ryan's wedding. They did not confirm or deny; Ryan and Jessica deserved privacy on their honeymoon. After he'd gone, Quinn suggested that the exaggerated media presence in town was due to the imminent arrival of the governor-general, who'd been invited to officiate at the annual ANZAC Day festivities. Dani peered at the article in the morning newspaper detailing the commemoration of Australian and New Zealand military action in WW1. "Every year they drag some poor old dignitary out at five in the morning." She grinned. "Not that I'm complaining since it's a public holiday."

"You don't admire Sir John?" Quinn asked.

Dani shrugged. "I don't particularly admire any politician."

"He's not a politician," Quinn pointed out. "He is the governor-general, the Queen's representative in this colony of ours."

"But he was prime minister once." Dani rolled her eyes. "What a lot of fuss. The mayor is putting on a posh reception at the Sea Temple. VIPs only. Three TV stations, local and national celebrities—and all for some boring old—"

Sonya sighed heavily and put her hand on her purse. Dani looked up from her paper.

"I'm going back to the hotel," her mother said,

pushing her chair out from the table. "I think I have one of my headaches coming on."

"I thought you wanted to see the shop." Dani had been looking forward to showing off her new spring pieces. She also had a surprise for her mother and for Quinn. Yesterday, she'd secured a lease for the bigger shop a few doors down from hers. Whatever Quinn thought about the location, Dani Hammond was on the way up.

But Sonya got to her feet, looking pale. "I'd rather see if we could leave a little earlier and get the flight over with as quickly as possible," she said apologetically.

"You were perfectly fine a minute ago," Dani pouted in the flurry of activity as everyone rose from the table. "We'll see you upstairs."

"No, it's fine. Take care, darling." She hugged her daughter tightly, whispering "I *do* like him" into Dani's ear. When she pulled back, Sonya's eyes were suspiciously brilliant. "But I love you," she whispered, touching her cheek, then was gone.

What was that about? Dani wondered, feeling a little uneasy. Her mother wasn't given to emotional goodbyes. Perhaps she was sick. That wasn't the first time she'd had a migraine when they'd been out.

Maybe she and Garth had had an argument….

"Perhaps she just had a little too much champagne last night," Quinn commented, practicing that weird way he had of seeming to see inside her head.

"Probably. I'll call her later."

They drove back to the beach house and Dani's mind

turned to other matters. "Now that the wedding is over, I'd better get busy on the necklace."

"Yes. And if you finish it on time," Quinn murmured, "I have a surprise for you. How would you like to strut the red carpet wearing something fabulous, be the envy of all your friends?"

Her eyes shone as he told her he had an invite to the governor-general's reception—"The one to honour some boring old—"

"True?" VIPs liked jewellery. What a showcase! "How did you get an invite?"

"He's a friend."

"Sir John is a friend?" Dani unfolded the paper on her lap and peered at the photo of an old guy in an old suit that boasted a row of medals.

Somehow she couldn't see him and Quinn out on the golf course together. "He's too old and too frail to be your friend."

"Not at all," Quinn demurred. "He's an avid collector. I trust his recommendations and judgement above any man I know. I've dealt with him for years."

This was a chance to meet someone close to Quinn. A chance to show off some of her pieces.

She sat back in her seat, already thinking that her lilac organza dress would be perfect for the occasion.

"*If* you get the necklace finished on time," Quinn warned.

The next two days, she closeted herself in her workroom, forbidding him to disturb her until she'd finished. Platinum was a fascinating metal, though it required a great deal of attention. As it was extremely pliable when heated, just one gram could be drawn to produce a fine wire more than two kilometres long. Luckily she didn't require quite that much. The cage she was making to encase the diamond was very delicate, but the density of platinum ensured its durability.

Finally it was done. Dani emerged, bleary-eyed, from the workroom to find Quinn sitting at breakfast, reading the paper. She glanced at the date on the paper, the twenty-fourth of April. The deadline was safe.

Quinn rose and picked up a cup from the tray on the table, concern in his eyes.

Dani stopped him as he picked up the coffeepot. "No, I'm going to bed."

"How's it coming?"

She hesitated, feeling almost nauseated with all the emotions raging inside. She was exhausted, relieved, cautiously optimistic that he'd like it. But mostly she wondered if this would be the end for them. "It's finished."

A small, slow smile appeared on his face. "Show me."

Dani backed away. "No, I'm too tired. And too nervous. You go look at it and formulate your hopefully complimentary comments later."

Quinn eased back into his chair. "All right. Get some sleep. I'll take you out somewhere nice tonight, just the two of us, to celebrate."

Dani nodded and climbed the stairs to bed.

Quinn walked into the workroom and immediately noticed that she'd tidied up. The workbench was swept clean, the tools stacked in their place. He thought how tired she'd looked and wondered if she had slept at all.

The necklace was up on its bust on the desk. Quinn switched the desk lamp on, pulled the chair well back and sat.

He was still there an hour later.

He looked first for impact, and got it in spades. A diamond inside a diamond. Mere filaments of platinum, like the gossamer wings of a dragonfly, held the huge trilliant-cut stone suspended inside a web cage. Platinum was the perfect setting for the intense yellow stone. It contained no alloys to tinge a diamond's brilliance and its reflective qualities enhanced the colour without distracting from it.

Quinn moved the bust from side to side to see every angle and put his judge's cap on. Innovative design, effective use of the gem, quality of workmanship, wearability. Ten out of ten in all categories. It was beautifully finished, totally professional, fresh and original.

And more conservative than he had originally feared, given her propensity for large, striking jewellery. The essence and personality of the diamond shone through, as a stone of this beauty and importance deserved.

Had she chosen this design, he wondered, as symbolic of herself, hiding in a cage of her own making? Was she brave enough to step into the limelight and let herself shine?

Quinn really was going to have to talk to her about moving to Sydney and marketing herself properly. His broker's brain started ticking. If this piece went to auction it would cause a stir. Just off the top of his head, he could think of three collectors who would pay a king's ransom for it.

But then he remembered. It wasn't going to auction. The owner of this necklace had quite a different purpose in mind.

That night, on their way out for dinner, Quinn placed the necklace around her neck and showed her what it looked like.

"Quinn, I can't," she protested, but her eyes were bright with excitement. "I'd be too nervous. What if someone sees?"

"Everyone should see, just for tonight." He tugged gently at her dangly angel earrings. "I think these are superfluous, don't you?"

She smiled at him in the mirror, her hand already reaching to dispatch the earrings. "You really like it?"

Quinn had spent the past couple of hours in bed with her showing her how much he liked it, but she deserved every indulgence. He nuzzled her bare shoulder, keeping his eyes on her reflection. "It is truly outstanding. *You* are truly outstanding."

He meant every word. It had come to him earlier in the workroom that he wanted to be the key to unlocking Dani's self-imposed cage. Throughout the day, waiting for her to wake up, he'd nurtured the idea, considered it, like the necklace, from every angle. More than that, he allowed himself to expand on practicalities, like geography, career, family. All the things he'd thought about in his apartment in Sydney.

Guilt had forced him to step back since then, but

Quinn was tired of denying it. He wanted to share in her life and wanted her to share in his. But there were still so many secrets and lies between them. Breaking Jake's confidence the other night had been about reassuring her, giving her something, because he knew he was about to inflict the most monstrous betrayal of all.

Over dinner, looking across the table at a masterpiece of design and the work of art wearing it, Quinn sought to be the perfect dinner companion, attentive and charming, as he knew she expected. But the food and wine were ashes in his mouth. He prayed her generous nature would forgive him.

Later he took her to his room and commanded her to strip until she wore only her high-heeled sandals and the necklace. He took the clip from her hair, letting it flow like a river of fire. Standing behind her as she peered into a mirror, he watched her face and saw that she, too, was struck by the beauty of her creation, and by the way her own beauty enhanced it.

He'd known she would look like this, but he drank the image in, in case it was all he'd have in the years to come. Her eyes mirrored the fire and sparkle of the intense yellow diamond, her irises ringed with gold. She moved her shoulders, a tiny repetitive sway from side to side, watching the diamond leap to life between her breasts. The perfect setting.

Quinn's large dark hands moved over her lush body, down the length of her torso, over the soft feminine curves of her bejewelled belly. He'd pulled the bed stool over in front of the mirror and now eased them down, bringing her slowly down onto him. Her legs parted and her eyes locked on his while he moved his hands over her, cupping her breasts, teasing her inside thighs, stroking her intimately. He made love to her tenderly, watching her hair ripple like firelight. The stone between her breasts changed the colour of her eyes to sheer, shimmering pleasure. When she shuddered and smiled her love and satisfaction back at him, he closed his eyes and allowed his release to engulf him in a wash of colourful ecstasy. And he knew he'd done the unthinkable. He had fallen in love with Dani Hammond.

Twelve

Sir John Knowles was tall and thin with drawn cheeks and a pallor of fatigue. She'd read somewhere he was in his early sixties, but from where she stood, Australia's most beloved statesman looked a lot older. To his right stood a birdlike woman, elegantly attired, her hands clasped tightly in front of her.

"Is that his wife?" Dani whispered to Quinn.

"Clare." Quinn volunteered nothing else.

Dani rolled her eyes and hoped he would loosen up a little once the formalities were out of the way. He'd barely spoken all day, except to reiterate how talented she was. She only hoped his client, whoever he or she was, thought so, too.

Quinn's approbation thrilled her except for an inexplicable feeling she could not define. It was nothing more noteworthy than his eyes sliding off hers just a fraction too soon, a watchfulness throughout the day, a hint of regret, even.

But then she remembered their lovemaking last night. Dani had never associated tenderness with this man, but last night she'd drowned in it, had truly felt special and cherished. Oh, there were logistical problems—the fact that he lived in Sydney, that he travelled constantly. But how could he make love to her so tenderly if he intended to leave her?

She rubbed her arms, pleased with her decision not to go with the summery organza dress. Her belted floral tunic, master-and-commander jacket and ankle boots might be a touch unconventional for a stuffy reception of this kind, but this was about exposure. The keishi-pearl-and-sapphire necklace was far too feminine to be trumped by lilac. It needed to rise above the bold, and triumph.

She fingered the necklace absently, looking down at the red carpet they inched forward on. As she did, she recalled the light in Quinn's eyes as she'd emerged from her bedroom earlier tonight.

"You always keep me guessing and you never disappoint," he'd said, giving her a little twirl.

Now Quinn's grip on her arm tightened and she realised they were at the front of the queue at last. He placed his hand over hers, staring resolutely ahead. The dignitary seemed to lose a little of his stoop when he saw them.

"Quinn," Sir John said simply, reaching out with both hands and clasping his.

"May I introduce—" she heard Quinn say as he tugged her forward "—Danielle Hammond."

Sir John took Dani's proffered hand and enclosed it with both of his. He stared down into her face for such a long time that she felt her smile stretch and become stale.

Quinn shook hands with Sir John's wife, then reached into his inside pocket and took out a long rectangular box. Ignoring Dani's wide-eyed comprehension, he offered it to the governor-general. With one last bony squeeze of her hand, Sir John released her and took the box from Quinn. Without opening it, he passed it to his wife.

Dani's smile froze. So the necklace—her necklace—was for Sir John, or at least his wife. The woman who smiled tentatively at her now.

Loss hit hard, followed by dread. It wasn't unusual to feel emotional when she sold a favourite piece, but right now she was just plain worried. Quinn had inferred she should make the necklace as if she were going to wear it. Somehow she couldn't imagine that necklace, that bold diamond, around this woman's neck.

Sir John turned back to her, and if he noticed her stricken expression, his calm smile didn't waver. "Thank you, my dear." He tilted his head at the jewellery box his wife held.

It's too young for you, Dani thought.

"Would you do me the honour," Sir John said, "of joining my wife and me for a drink in our suite in a little while?"

Quinn answered for both of them. "Of course, Sir John."

Dani could barely contain herself until they were out of earshot. "I don't believe it! He's your client?"

Quinn nodded, directing her over to a waiter with a tray of drinks.

"Oh, Quinn," she whispered loudly. "You encouraged me to make something contemporary. Something I would wear myself." She shook her head, very worried. "It's too young for her."

He handed her a glass of wine. "Dani, the necklace is perfect."

"But…" If only he'd told her, given her a picture of the woman or something. "She'd prefer brilliants all over it, possibly other gems, or pearls… Damn it, I should have gone for pearls."

Quinn took a long sip of wine, then tipped her chin up with his finger. "Sir John knows jewellery. He will see exactly what I see. You're world class, Dani Hammond, in every way."

Her nerves calmed somewhat. She trusted him. Quinn had too much integrity to let her fall flat on her face. His own professional reputation was at stake, too.

It was still a tense hour and a half until the mayor appeared and requested they follow him. And she still crossed her fingers on the way.

The mayor waved them into a luxurious suite and then left. Sir John and his wife sat on one of two settees. Behind them, French doors opened out onto a large balcony. Dani caught a glimpse of twinkling blue water from the lighted pool below.

On a coffee table between the settees sat the open blue velvet box.

Sir John rose and came to greet them, his smile born of real warmth rather than the restrained politeness of the reception. He seemed a little younger than before, more sprightly, and hugged Quinn, who warmly reciprocated. Then he led Dani to the settee.

She felt too nervous to accept a drink. Mrs. Knowles sat staring at the necklace while the two men made a little small talk. Then they sat, too.

An awkward silence descended. Everyone's eyes seemed to gravitate toward the open jewellery box. Quinn sat beside her, his shoulders back, as tense as Dani had ever seen him. He didn't look at her once.

Her eyes moved restlessly from one to the other, wishing someone would speak. After at least a minute of this, she began to pray for the floor to open up and swallow her. Finally she couldn't take the tension a moment longer. "Is something wrong with the necklace?" she blurted out.

Quinn grasped her hand, still without looking at her. She heard Mrs. Knowles clear her throat and murmur something that sounded ominously like "Poor child."

Sir John lifted his head wearily, fixed his wife and then Quinn with a stern look and said quietly, "Would you leave us?"

Mrs. Knowles rose quickly, looking at Quinn. With a last squeeze of her hand, Quinn rose. Bemused, Dani, too, started to rise.

But Quinn laid a heavy hand on her shoulder, pushing her gently back down. "Stay," he murmured, giving her shoulder a firm squeeze.

She subsided, completely confused now. Quinn and Mrs. Knowles left the room together and closed the door quietly.

What the hell is going on?

An ominous foreboding swamped her. If he didn't like the necklace, why couldn't he just say? She could change it, fix it; he was paying enough. She'd be happy to consult with his wife on the design.

Dani looked longingly at the closed door, wishing she was on the other side. With Quinn.

"He's a good man," Sir John said quietly, following her gaze.

She settled back in the seat, calling on all her composure. "Is your wife unhappy with the necklace?"

Kindly hazel eyes searched her face. He was very tall, as tall as Quinn, but his clothes and his skin looked like he'd lost weight in a hurry. "Clare thinks, as I do, that you're very gifted. But—" he cleared his throat and leaned forward "—the necklace is not for Clare." He picked up the open box and held it out to her. "It's for you."

She must have misheard. "Sorry?"

The box shook quite markedly in the old man's hands so she sat forward and put her hands on it to steady it.

"Quinn found the diamond for me six years ago, you know." His voice became a little less thready, a little warmer. "I always intended you to have it."

They sat there both holding the box in midair until he pushed it gently into her hands and she had no choice but to take it.

"You're starting to scare me, Sir John."

The man took a deep breath, looking earnestly into her face. "This is my apology and my legacy to you, Danielle, for I am your father."

I am your father.

Dani lowered the box slowly to her lap, her lips moving soundlessly. *Her father.* The two words chased each other around her head. Of all the things she might have expected at this glittering occasion, this was not one of them. And why didn't Quinn tell her? Did he know?

A piercing pain in her chest confirmed his betrayal. Of course he knew. He'd set her up.

Her father. She searched his face, thinking there must be some kind of connection, some kind of familiarity, surely. A proud nose, pockmarked with age and infirmity. A still-strong chin but sunken cheeks that whispered of pain. His bow tie seemed too tight around his scrawny neck, wormed with loose flesh. A plain white shirt covered what looked to be a wasted chest.

Dani stopped searching. There was nothing of her in this old man. She'd walk past him on the street and not feel the slightest hint of recognition. She wouldn't look at him twice.

A lump of anger slowly formed, not just toward him but Quinn as well. And her mother. She must have known this was coming. Dani let it burn just under the surface, wondering if he could see it on her staring face.

Sir John must have realised he wasn't going to get any help from her. He picked up his glass and sipped.

"I was the leader of the opposition. Your mother, Sonya," he said, his voice caressing the word, causing Dani to suck in air, "was helping out in the campaign office."

She swallowed heavily but managed to keep quiet.

"I was recently married to Clare, whom I'd known all my life. I noticed Sonya, I own to it. We were friends but nothing would have happened, for we were not bad people. I took my marriage vows seriously, and your mother was not the type of woman to wreck a marriage."

Don't tell me what my mother is, she wanted to snarl. *Don't even speak her name.* But she held her tongue.

"But then your aunt Ursula died. Your mother was inconsolable. I'd tried so hard to keep away from her. We'd both tried. The consequences were much more serious than my marriage, my career. I would have risked that happily for Sonya. But it was the party, the one that was going to take the country into the new decade…."

Dani had a sudden and savage insight into why she hated politicians, the way they tried to justify everything.

Sir John closed his eyes. "I intended only to offer comfort, but one thing led to another. She fell pregnant almost immediately."

In the dead silence that followed, a million questions and accusations swamped her. She knew she had to consider those different times, her mother's unenviable situation, the lure of a powerful, charismatic man. Heck, she was no angel herself. But her anger seemed to suck up her compassion for now. She'd get to it later, away from here.

"I loved her very much," the old man said plaintively. "Please never doubt that."

Her heartbeat sounded in her ears, loud, slow,

ominous. "Sure you did," she said softly, feeling the hot breath of her anger like fire in her throat. "That's why you kept in such close contact."

He closed his eyes briefly, his thin lips drawn in a slash of anguish. "I don't expect you to understand, but I am more sorry than you will ever know."

Dani clenched her teeth and looked down at the necklace. So sorry he was buying her off. Didn't he know she came cheap? A cup of coffee would have done, a bunch of flowers on her birthday or graduation. A simple phone call.

"I've thought about you every day." His voice was high and thin.

But not enough to get in touch. Her hand seemed to jerk up of its own accord, jabbing toward the balcony. "How fortuitous the ANZAC Day commemoration was up here this year. After twenty-seven years, you could kill two birds with one stone."

Sir John took a long time answering. "I'm so sorry, my dear. I wanted very much to be part of your life, but it wasn't possible. You see, Howard blackmailed me to keep away."

No. He wouldn't. A huge fist closed around her chest. Please say it's not true…. "Wh-why, what possible reason…?"

"The miners had been on strike for two years. The government was making a bad fist of it." His pallor became even more washed out and he inhaled deeply. "Industry was being crippled. My party promised to crush the strikers. Howard—all industry leaders—could not afford for us to fail."

And an affair outside marriage, a teenage pregnancy in those days would have been the death knell for the party.

How could Howard do it? She wanted to moan and scream with rage and betrayal. What right did he have? She wrapped her arms around her middle, still holding the jewellery box.

"I'm so sorry," the old man—her father—whispered, and she tried, she really did, to dredge up some compassion. But the rage was hot and hard and impossible to swallow.

"I'm dying, Danielle. Lung cancer."

The words hung in the air between them while she clutched herself, rocking. His eyes beseeched her.

Her brain was going into overload. He was dying. He wasn't here because he wanted to meet her, to get to know the bastard daughter. He was here to assuage his guilt before the end.

She couldn't breathe. The keishi necklace dug into her throat and the anger coursing through her wasn't hot and hard anymore. It was stone-cold fury.

Dani stood abruptly, holding the jewellery box. "How dare you!" And without any rational thought at all, just a need to rage, she threw the box at the wall behind him. It hit with a dull *thwack*, bounced off the cabinet and fell to the floor. The platinum cage holding the diamond glittered, the chain spilled out onto the white tiles.

"You selfish old…" Some kind of insane respect stopped her from saying the word *bastard*. He was after all, the governor-general of Australia.

Sir John remained seated, his head bowed, his sunken cheeks even more pronounced and impossibly pale. But she didn't care. She jerked into action, heard the quick, sharp click of her heels, and then she wrenched the door open and ran smack into Quinn's chest.

How dare he as well?

Dani reeled away, putting her hands up in front of her like a shield.

He spoke her name, took her wrists gently, and it required a superhuman effort not to slap him away, or slap his face.

Clare Knowles slipped past them and into the suite, looking very upset.

"How could you?" Dani demanded in a strangled moan. "How could you do this to me?"

"Dani, I'm so sorry."

"Let me go."

He tugged her toward a chair. "I had to. He's dying."

She resisted his efforts to sit her down. "How long have you known?"

Quinn swallowed and looked away. "Since the day we left Sydney."

Dani bit down on the inside of her mouth. She remembered the phone call, his polite excuse "I have to take this…" She had gone on to the airstrip without him.

She tasted blood. "You bastard," she said quietly.

He jerked his head toward the suite where presumably Sir John was being comforted by his wife. "Howard Blackstone was blackmailing him to keep away."

"Don't!" Her voice cracked. "Don't even speak his name. Howard was twice the man you will ever be."

He rolled his head back and sighed. "Dani, he's dying. He's my friend and he begged me and he's dying." He kneaded her hands between his.

"I told you the other night my father meant nothing to me. God, Quinn, we *talked* about it. You had a golden opportunity to tell me."

"Would you have come if I'd told you?"

She shook her head, trying to pull out of his grasp. "You set me up. I don't know how you could do that, take me in there and leave me." The tears started in earnest now and she was ashamed. Ashamed of crying, of upsetting an old man.

Of believing in Quinn Everard.

"I thought I loved you, but I couldn't love someone who could do that," she sobbed, her hands still imprisoned in his grasp. "I hate you."

"Quinn?" Clare Knowles stood in the doorway.

Dani turned her head away, not wanting to see or be seen by the woman, even as she registered the worry in her voice. But it was the slide of Quinn's stricken eyes from her face to the other woman's that gave her the will, the strength to push away from him.

Once again, she was second in line, never number one. Not good enough to be a daughter. Not good enough to be a Blackstone. Not good enough to be a fiancée.

Not good enough to be his…

Thirteen

Late on a public holiday Friday, the streets thronged with inebriated activity. Shortly after storming out on Quinn and her father, Dani stood outside her shop, looking in, drowning in self-pity and hating herself for it. How could Quinn do it to her, allow her to walk into the most important moment of her life unprepared?

And her mother—she had a lot to answer for. With a flash of anger, Dani pulled her phone from her purse and dialed. Sonya cried, saying she had dreaded this moment since learning of the official visit a few weeks ago.

"John called me a couple of weeks after Howard's funeral, wanting to contact you. I said no, you were happy, I begged him." She knew nothing of Howard's blackmail, but admitted that it was Howard who told her the leader of the opposition wanted nothing to do with her or her baby. "He gave me a choice: the stigma and scandal of bringing down the next government, or security. He said he would always take care of us. I had to do the right thing for you."

"Did you love him?" Dani asked tremulously. "My father?"

"I thought I did." Her mother sighed. "You have to understand, I was just nineteen. Overnight my life changed from being a carefree teen to suddenly being responsible for two kids, because Howard was so dev- astated by Ursula's death, he wasn't coping. John was kind, attractive, important."

Her mother begged to come up first thing in the morning, but Dani knew she was far too low to resist the coddling and entreaties to bring her home to Sydney. She asked for a few days' grace and hung up.

A group of people came out of a bar, weaving across the road, then scattering to let a screaming ambulance pass. Her reflection in the window fractured, just like her heart, and she knew she needed the sanctuary of the beach. At this time of night, it would be deserted.

She walked aimlessly onto the dunes toward Four Mile. There was no hurry; self-pity was a leisurely activity. The events of her day, her life, flashed through her mind, keeping her company.

An unworthy man had asked her at the ripe old age of twenty-five to marry him, and she'd accepted because he'd asked. All she wanted was to be the apple of someone's eye, the centrepiece. That episode had dented her heart, and now it had happened again. And what she'd felt for Nick was pathetic compared to her love for Quinn Everard. It was the difference between being strapped into a wheelchair in the rain or walking on the beach on a sunny day.

It was a bad night for the men in her life, she thought bitterly. A long-lost father who'd never acknowledged or contacted her had finally appeared, only to tell her he was dying. Her cherished benefactor had cruelly betrayed her and her memories of him would be tarnished forever. And the man she'd fallen heart and soul in love with had not uttered a single truth since the day they'd met.

The waves soothed her, as always. The beach was her friend. She knew every palm, every half-buried log, every crevice in the iron-grey sand.

Pushing Quinn from her thoughts, she cajoled her brain to accept and get used to two words. My father. My father, the governor-general. My father who is dying. The man whose nonexistence had shaped the way she felt about herself.

Which was, for the most part, not good enough.

But her feelings of inadequacy weren't his fault. Had she not had every advantage in life? She hadn't grown up on the streets like the kids that Quinn and his parents took in. She'd enjoyed a luxurious home, the best schools. Hell, she hadn't even had to raise the money to start her own business. Howard had handed it to her on a plate.

A pretty stone winked up at her in the moonlight. With her booted foot, she kicked it and watched as it skittered away in a satisfying arc. Okay, she had reason to be angry and hurt that everyone had lied. Her mother.

Howard. Her father. Quinn. But she could snack on self-pity till the cows came home. It was still a meager meal.

Her father's sad face swam in front of her eyes. How could she not even have given him a chance to explain? How long did he have left? Twenty-seven years and it all came down to this, compressed into a bitter pill of recrimination.

Oh God, what if the upset tonight had triggered a turn for the worse? Dani quickened her step, suddenly not aimless anymore. She couldn't turn her back on him, not when she didn't know him. Not when he was the one person she had missed all her life.

She was at the halfway point between town and Four Mile, another twenty minutes to either, if she ran. What if she was too late? Her breath came in gasps as she broke into a jog. She was so immersed in her prayers and panic, she didn't even hear the motorbike until it was nearly on top of her.

"Dani! Get on!"

What on earth? Quinn, tux and all on a filthy, mud-streaked dirt bike.

"Stop, damn you!"

Dani stopped, her chest heaving with exertion and amazement. He ripped off his helmet and thrust it out to her, his mouth a grim line.

She hadn't even begun thinking about Quinn, where he fit in her life now.

"Get on," he repeated urgently. "He's been rushed to Cairns Base Hospital."

With a cry of dismay, she shoved the helmet over her

curls and clambered awkwardly onto the back of the bike. She wrapped her arms around him as they gathered speed, squeezed her eyes shut and prayed for all she was worth.

Less than an hour later, they screeched to a halt at the entrance to the hospital.

"Go. I'll meet you in there."

Chilled to the bone by cold and worry, she rushed to find her father.

To her intense relief, Sir John had suffered a mild respiratory attack due to excess fluid on his lungs, a common symptom of advanced lung cancer, she learned. He was awake and fairly comfortable and would be kept overnight for observation, but would be discharged in the morning.

Dani spent the next hour sitting beside him, her hand covering his. He gazed at her, unable to speak because of the oxygen mask, but he turned his hand up and squeezed hers and even smiled once. His wife sat opposite and told them both that he must take the next few days away from official duties to spend some time with his daughter.

It was after 3:00 a.m. when Dani left the emergency unit. She was exhausted, rumpled and grimy and had no idea where she was going to spend the night. She certainly didn't expect Quinn to be sitting in the waiting room.

Despite everything, her heart warmed at the sight of him, his tuxedo crumpled, black hair standing on end. A far cry from the sophisticate who'd escorted her up the red carpet earlier in the evening.

That seemed a lifetime ago, so much had happened. So much had changed.

"How is he?" His eyes were rimmed with weariness and worry.

"Resting. They're keeping him in overnight, but he can go back to the hotel tomorrow."

"To the hotel?" He looked surprised. "Not home?"

"They've decided to stick around Port for a few days." She sat down, leaving a couple of seats between them.

"I see." He looked glad for her. "Is that good?" His head lowered and tilted, his eyes turned up under his brows.

Dani gave a tired smile and nodded. "That's good."

She took a deep breath and repeated the words in her mind. It was good. She had a lot of lost time to make up for. So did her father, and she was going to make sure he did.

"Can you explain how you came to be riding a motorbike on Four Mile Beach in the middle of the night?"

Quinn scrubbed at the dark shadow chasing his jaw line. "I initially thought you'd be at the shop, but then I remembered the beach."

He'd remembered. Her special place. "And the bike?"

His hand moved to his hair as he tried to repair the damage an hour of speeding on a motorbike in cool, damp air had inflicted. "An interesting sequence of events involving four boys messing about on the beach, my Rolex, a few bucks and a few choice threats." His mouth quirked. "Not to mention the possibility of being arrested at any minute."

Dani laughed shakily. "My hero."

My hero, the liar. Her smile faded.

So did his. "I thought you'd never forgive yourself if…" He nodded toward the emergency unit.

"That's why I started running," she murmured. "On the beach." She paused. "Thank you." It sounded wholly inadequate, but Dani didn't know what else to say.

There was an awkward silence. She rubbed her arms briskly, grateful again for her jacket and boots. Imagine the bike ride in her organza dress.

"Dani," he said softly, his eyes tormented. "I'm so sorry I hurt you like that."

She looked away. Did she want to hear it? Could she trust him, after all the lies he'd told? His were pretty big lies, after all. Not "You look lovely" or "Of course I didn't forget your birthday…" His lies involved blackmail, enticement, shady business goings-on, concealing a father.

But after all the crying and all the emotions of the evening, her anger had drained away.

Her sadness had not. "I know why you did it," she began. "You couldn't give your wife her dying wish. This was another chance."

"A chance to even the score," he mused. "You might be right. I figured I had the time to make it up to you. Your father is nearly out of time."

To make it up to her? He was asking a lot. "We've established that you're a loyal friend, then. Maybe not such a loyal lover."

Pain darkened his eyes even more. "I think I can be. It's not love for Laura that has stopped me falling in love these past few years. I didn't need it and I didn't miss it. I lived well, travelled incessantly, made a lot of money." He shifted forward in his seat, exhaling noisily. "I thought I was happy. Being alone, pleasing myself. I thought I had it all together. But you…"

"I what?" Her pulse skipped, but then, being in the same country as Quinn Everard made her pulse skip. Was he saying he wanted her, that it wasn't over?

"I won't lose you," he said fiercely, grasping her hands, "not when you've turned my life upside down."

She gently pried her hands loose and twisted them in her lap. A great wave of emotion and exhaustion blocked her ability to make sense of anything. Lord, it had been a long day, but she needed to focus. Did he mean he wanted to change his life for her? That he was interested in a relationship?

There was movement in the corner of her eye. Quinn Everard sat two feet away, fidgeting. The great nego-tiator who had calmly tossed away fifteen million English pounds on a painting, without so much as a muscle twitch, was fidgeting.

"You said you loved me," he muttered through clenched teeth.

"Did I?" Yes, she remembered, at the reception before storming out. "I also said I hated you."

"I wasn't looking for this, but then I found you." He turned to face her and grasped her wrists again before she could snatch them away. "You found me. I love you, Dani. I didn't want to, I tried not to, but I do."

Her head jerked up, but somehow she kept her hands calmly, quietly in his. "You—you love me?" She searched his face for guilt or pity.

Quinn sighed gustily. "Dani, you're smart, funny, vibrant. You're bloody frustrating and incredibly talented. I think about you every second, and when I'm not with you, I miss you, your smile and your colour." He spoke quickly, urgently. "You're the only person in more years than I care to think about who's made me feel this way." He lifted and shook her hands gently. "The only person who's *ever* made me feel this way."

"Oh." Her tongue seemed to be stuck to the roof of her mouth. Light-headed with surprise and excitement and love, she swayed drunkenly, hoping she wasn't about to pass out. The light in his eyes made her dizzy with hope but still afraid to believe what she saw in them. Afraid to trust in the love that shone out.

Quinn leaned forward and brushed her cheek with his thumb, and she realised she was crying. "Can you forgive me, sweetheart? I'll gladly spend the rest of my life making it up to you."

She dug her nails into his palms as joy swelled inside. Could it be true that everything she'd ever wanted was within her grasp?

And he was everything she'd ever wanted. Sexy as hell and well-respected everywhere. Loyal and warm toward those he loved. Encouraging and motivated about her work. She'd loved him, probably since the moment she set eyes on him, but definitely since Sydney. "I fell in love with you in Sydney," she blurted, finishing on a big sniff.

"I wanted you to come to my place, meet my people and see where we went from there. But I don't think I actually accepted it as love until the other night when I broke a promise to Jake. And then, when I saw the necklace…"

He shifted over to the seat between them and enfolded her in his arms. "You're dead on your feet."

Dani sniffed again, rubbing her wet face on his lapel. "How are we going to do this?" she whimpered. "You live down there. You travel all the time…."

His mouth moved on her hair and he tightened his grip. "I have a plan. Half the year up here—the cooler half, if you don't mind—and the other in Sydney. Steve runs the shop and when we're up here in Port, you design." He pulled back and tipped her face up, looking down at her sternly. "Then we go all out to promote you in Sydney, Dani. The whole works, launches, publicity, celebrity photo shoots. It's time to stop running, to show everyone what you're made of."

"Okay," she said cautiously. "But what about your business?"

Quinn shrugged. "That's what staff are for. I'll cut back on the travel, except for those trips where you can come, too, and tout your stuff in the big centres."

She closed her eyes, leaning into his warmth, so tired yet awash with exhilaration.

With Quinn beside her, she would never be afraid of success or failure again. She would reach for the stars, stamp number one on everything she touched. He would continually push her to be the best, and that's what she wanted, more than anything else.

Dani's heart burst with joy, even as she felt her eyes drifting closed. She came first for him; she was his precious jewel. Her father wanted her around for the limited time he had left. Her cousins would hopefully forge new bonds through the younger generation. Love and family, and all in such a short time.

She belonged.

* * * * *

Don't miss the next
DIAMONDS DOWN UNDER *title.*
Watch for
BOARDROOMS & A BILLIONAIRE HEIR
by Paula Roe, on sale this May
from Silhouette Desire.

Look for LAST WOLF WATCHING
by Rhyannon Byrd—the exciting conclusion in the
BLOODRUNNERS *miniseries*
from Silhouette Nocturne.

Follow Michaela and Brody on their fierce journey
to find the truth and face the demons from the past,
as they reach the heart of the battle between
the Runners and the rogues.

Here is a sneak preview of book three,
LAST WOLF WATCHING.

Michaela squinted, struggling to see through the impenetrable darkness. Everyone looked toward the Elders, but she knew Brody Carter still watched her. Michaela could feel the power of his gaze. Its heat. Its strength. And something that felt strangely like anger, though he had no reason to have any emotion toward her. Strangers from different worlds, brought together beneath the heavy silver moon on a night made for hell itself. That was their only connection.

The second she finished that thought, she knew it was a lie. But she couldn't deal with it now. Not tonight. Not when her whole world balanced on the edge of destruction.

Willing her backbone to keep her upright, Michaela Doucet focused on the towering blaze of a roaring bonfire that rose from the far side of the clearing, its orange flames burning with maniacal zeal against the inky black curtain of the night. Many of the Lycans had already shifted into their preternatural shapes, their fur-covered bodies standing like monstrous shadows at the edges of the forest as they waited with restless expectancy for her brother.

Her nineteen-year-old brother, Max, had been attacked by a rogue werewolf—a Lycan who preyed upon humans for food. Max had been bitten in the attack, which meant he was no longer human, but a breed of creature that existed between the two worlds of man and beast, much like the Bloodrunners themselves.

The Elders parted, and two hulking shapes emerged from the trees. In their wolf forms, the Lycans stood over seven feet tall, their legs bent at an odd angle as they stalked forward. They each held a thick chain that had been wound around their inside wrists, the twin lengths leading back into the shadows. The Lycans had taken no more than a few steps when they jerked on the chains, and her brother appeared.

Bound like an animal.

Biting at her trembling lower lip, she glanced left, then right, surprised to see that others had joined her. Now the Bloodrunners and their family and friends stood as a united force against the Silvercrest pack, which had yet to accept the fact that something sinister was eating away at its foundation—something that would rip down the protective walls that separated their world from the humans'. It occurred to Michaela that loyalties were being announced tonight—a separation made between those who would stand with the Runners in their fight against the rogues and those who blindly supported the pack's refusal to face reality. But all she could focus on was her brother. Max looked so hurt…so terrified.

"Leave him alone," she screamed, her soft-soled, black satin slip-ons struggling for purchase in the damp earth as she rushed toward Max, only to find herself lifted off the ground when a hard, heavily muscled arm clamped around her waist from behind, pulling her clear off her feet. "Damn it, let me down!" she snarled, unable to take her eyes off her brother as the golden-eyed Lycan kicked him.

Mindless with heartache and rage, Michaela clawed at the arm holding her, kicking her heels against whatever part of her captor's legs she could reach. "Stop it," a deep, husky voice grunted in her ear. "You're not helping him by losing it. I give you my word he'll survive the ceremony, but you have to keep it together."

"Nooooo!" she screamed, too hysterical to listen to reason. "You're monsters! All of you! Look what you've done to him! How dare you! *How dare you!*"

The arm tightened with a powerful flex of muscle, cinching her waist. Her breath sucked in on a sharp, wailing gasp.

"Shut up before you get both yourself and your brother killed. I will *not* let that happen. Do you understand me?" her captor growled, shaking her so hard that her teeth clicked together. "Do you understand me, Doucet?"

"Damn it," she cried, stricken as she watched one of the guards grab Max by his hair. Around them Lycans huffed and growled as they watched the spectacle, while others outright howled for the show to begin.

"That's enough!" the voice seethed in her ear. "They'll tear you apart before you even reach him, and I'll be damned if I'm going to stand here and watch you die."

Suddenly, through the haze of fear and agony and outrage in her mind, she finally recognised who'd caught her. *Brody.*

He held her in his arms, her body locked against his powerful form, her back to the burning heat of his chest. A low, keening sound of anguish tore through her, and her head dropped forward as hoarse sobs of pain ripped from her throat. "Let me go. I have to help him. *Please,*" she begged brokenly, knowing only that she needed to get to Max. "Let me go, Brody."

He muttered something against her hair, his breath warm against her scalp, and Michaela could have sworn it was a single word.... But she must have heard wrong. She was too upset. Too furious. Too terrified. She must be out of her mind.

Because it sounded as if he'd quietly snarled the word *never.*

HARLEQUIN® Romance®

Western Weddings

Jason Welborn was convinced that his business
partner's daughter, Jenny, had come to claim her share
in the business. But Jenny seemed determined to win
him over, and the more he tried to push her away, the
more feisty Jenny's response. Slowly but surely she
was starting to get under Jason's skin....

Look for

Coming Home to the Cattleman

by

JUDY CHRISTENBERRY

Available May wherever you buy books.

HRI7511

nocturne™

THE FINAL INSTALLMENT OF
THE BLOODRUNNERS TRILOGY

Last Wolf Watching

Runner Brody Carter has found his match in
Michaela Doucet, a human with unusual psychic powers.
When Michaela's brother is threatened, Brody becomes
her protector, and suddenly not only has to protect her
from her enemies but also from himself....

LOOK FOR
LAST WOLF WATCHING
BY
RHYANNON
BYRD

Available May 2008 wherever you buy books.

Dramatic and Sensual Tales of Paranormal Romance

www.eHarlequin.com   SN61786

REQUEST YOUR FREE BOOKS!

2 FREE NOVELS
PLUS 2
FREE GIFTS!

Passionate, Powerful, Provocative!

COMING NEXT MONTH

**#1867 BOARDROOMS & A BILLIONAIRE HEIR—
Paula Roe**
Diamonds Down Under
She'd been blackmailed into spying on Sydney's most infamous
corporate raider. Until he turned the tables and seduced her into a
marriage of convenience.

#1868 FALLING FOR KING'S FORTUNE—Maureen Child
Kings of California
This millionaire playboy was about to enter a loveless marriage
sure to make his wallet bigger...until a woman he'd never met
claimed to be the mother of his child.

#1869 MISTRESS FOR A MONTH—Ann Major
He will stop at nothing to get her inheritance. But her price is for
her to become his mistress...for a month.

#1870 DANTE'S STOLEN WIFE—Day Leclaire
The Dante Legacy
The curse of *The Inferno* left this billionaire determined to
make her his bride...and he doesn't care that she's his own twin
brother's fiancée.

#1871 SHATTERED BY THE CEO—Emilie Rose
The Payback Affairs
To fulfill the terms of his father's will, a business tycoon must
convince his former love to work for his company—and try to find
a way to stay out of her bed.

#1872 THE DESERT LORD'S BABY—Olivia Gates
Throne of Judar
He must marry and produce an heir if he is to become king.
But he doesn't know his ex-lover has already given birth to his
child....